"You think I'm making the ghost up."

Hayley glowered at Grant, her hair mussed, her expression one of pure rage.

Grant attempted to sidestep her question by trapping her in his arms on the bed.

She pushed him away before he could kiss her. "It turns you on to think I'm so insecure that I'd manufacture a ghost to call me names, to harass me about having carnal thoughts? Just so I could get your sympathy?"

With lightning-swift movements, he rolled over on her, pinning her to the mattress. "What turns me on is the way you look at me, the way you respond to me. With all due respect, Ms. Addison, it's in spite of your damned ghost—not because of him."

Readers loved Rita Award-winning author **Glenda Sanders**'s T # 316 *Dark Secrets* and T # 402 *Haunting Secrets* so much, that we couldn't resist asking Glenda to write one more heartfelt, suspense-packed, unforgettable romance featuring destined lovers whose love is threatened by tormented ghosts and a haunted house! And here it is...*Lovers' Secrets*. While Glenda's fondest dream is to live in a house by a lake—just like the one in her novel—with an office overlooking the water, she sincerely hopes that if she ever realizes this ambition, she will not discover that her dream house is haunted!

Books by Glenda Sanders

HARLEQUIN TEMPTATION
356—A HUMAN TOUCH
383—BABY CAKES
402—HAUNTING SECRETS
437—DR. HUNK

LOVERS' SECRETS

GLENDA SANDERS

Harlequin Books

TORONTO • NEW YORK • LONDON
AMSTERDAM • PARIS • SYDNEY • HAMBURG
STOCKHOLM • ATHENS • TOKYO • MILAN
MADRID • WARSAW • BUDAPEST • AUCKLAND

Published August 1993

ISBN 0-373-25554-3

LOVERS' SECRETS

THE LOUNGE CHAIR had been a good investment, Hayley thought, as she sank deeper into the plush cushions of her new acquisition. She'd been stretched out there since dusk, surveying her empire through the screen walls of the porch the locals referred to as a Florida room, and listening to the sounds of the night.

She hadn't a clue what creatures generated the separate sounds that blended into this symphony of night, the chirping, croaking, cawing, rustling, lapping and splashing that composed the nocturnal symphony. A woman who'd been raised on New York's Upper East Side couldn't be expected to know; the sounds of nature were markedly different from the cacophony of grinding car engines, squeaking brakes, sirens, televisions, boom boxes, and human voices of every pitch and volume which had been the raucous background music of her first twenty-four years of life.

The full moon cast a mellow glow over the lawn, turning shrubs into hunkering masses and trees into long-armed giants reaching toward the infinite, starless sky. Next winter her relatives would descend on her, escaping the cold and hard freeze of the northern winters, and her nieces and nephews would cavort on that lawn between the inevitable visits to Disney World and the Space Center.

By then, she should have the guest room furnished and a sleeper sofa for the living room.

Hayley smiled from the sheer pleasure of having her own place. Who would have thought that a woman who'd never lived anywhere but an apartment surrounded by family would have her own home with a spare bedroom and a tree-strewn lawn? Certainly not her parents, who'd viewed her decision to transfer south with her employer as an act of treasonous folly, instead of recognizing it for the declaration of independence that it was. They'd predicted only doom, gloom and homesickness when their baby girl flew the nest.

But here she was—the Addison family rebel, determined to prove them wrong—with her own car, her own house and property—and even a lake.

Lovers' Lake. Named for a couple who'd eloped in the dead of night in a row boat, the body of water appeared dark and deep and brooding in the moonlight, as though it held vast secrets in its depths. From her perch on the chaise, Hayley imagined that long-ago couple, madly in love and full of dreams, drifting across the water in the small boat on their way to "happily ever after."

Her fanciful ruminations were interrupted by a flash of headlights and the crunch of tires on the packed sand road that branched off the highway and continued past her house to the bait shop perched on the water's edge. Hayley's scalp prickled. The real estate agent had warned that there might be traffic on the road early in the morning once the bait shop had reopened, but who would be going to a bait shop after dark? Especially one that had been closed for over a year?

Hayley toyed with the idea of calling the police, then chided herself for overreacting. She might be living by herself for the first time in her life. She might be living in an isolated house on a lake instead of in a noisy apartment building. But she wasn't going to jump at every noise, or call the police every time a car made a wrong turn off the highway. She was safe enough there on the porch hidden in the shadows.

The intruding vehicle was a pickup truck. It stopped in front of the bait store, and the engine sputtered to silence with a mechanical flatulence that would have sent Hayley in search of an automotive shop had she owned the vehicle. The door opened with a protesting screech of metal against metal, and the driver hopped out of the cab and slammed the door.

Whoever he was—even in the pale moonlight, the figure was unmistakably male—he was obviously unconcerned about making noise. But his lack of caution was hardly reassuring to Hayley. Few people knew her house was occupied, and anyone familiar with the area might assume there was no one near enough to hear. She was grateful for the shadows that hid her.

The interloper moved with the graceful coordination of the physically fit as he strode toward the shop and ascended the concrete steps to the porch that spanned the width of the building.

Hayley tensed as he lifted the padlock on the door. *Was he breaking in?* If so, he was proficient. Within seconds, the door was open, and the mystery man had disappeared into the frame building.

Hayley pushed herself into a sitting position, ready to dash inside and call the police. A wrong turn was one thing, breaking and entering quite another. But just as she lowered her feet to the floor, light flooded through the shop windows and splashed across the narrow porch.

Feeling both relieved and foolish, Hayley relaxed back into the cushions of the chaise longue. Someone had had the power turned on at the bait shop. Obviously, her mysterious intruder was the new owner the real estate agent had told her about, Grant Mackenzie. No wonder he hadn't been concerned about noise!

With the lights on, the interior of the shop was clearly visible through the windows. A maze of sheet-draped cartons and display cases filled the room, and Hayley watched as the new proprietor moved from one spot to another, lifting the corners of tarps to peek and poke curiously at the contents. After several minutes, he leaned against the main counter, crossed his arms over his waist and surveyed the room.

Was that rise and fall of chest a sigh of satisfaction or dismay? Hayley couldn't tell from the distance. She was beginning to feel slightly voyeuristic observing her new neighbor without his knowledge, but she was more than a little curious about Grant Mackenzie.

The bait shop had been built by the previous owner of her house, a retiree from New Jersey who had run the shop for several years before his death. Hayley had assumed the new buyer was retired too, but the man she could see so clearly through the window wasn't old enough to be even halfway to standard retirement age. Fit and sturdily built, he was wearing close-fitting jeans—and filling them out very well. His thick, tawny-gold hair mocked the graying and thinning of age. If first impressions were any indication, Grant Mackenzie could turn out to be a very interesting neighbor.

He leaned pensively against the counter for several minutes. Then, with a purposeful squaring of his shoulders, he straightened and walked outside to his truck. He dropped the tailgate, then paused and regarded the boxes and suitcases loaded on the truck bed.

The proper thing to do, Hayley decided, would be to go introduce herself as any neighbor should. He might appreciate some help with the boxes, or a hot cup of coffee.

And then again, he might not. With his back to Hayley, he was but a dark silhouette, but something about the set of those wide shoulders and the forward tilt of his head bespoke restless energy and a troubled state of mind. There was something unsettling—and unwelcoming—about his periods of absolute stillness. She knew nothing about Grant Mackenzie beyond his name and it might not be wise to barge in on a stranger at this time of night, when she wasn't sure he would welcome company.

On the other hand, it was silly to sit in the dark spying on the man. After all, they *were* neighbors, and they were going to meet sooner or later. It might as well be now, when she could offer a helping hand. Maybe if she carried in a few boxes, she could cajole him into hanging the mirror she'd bought for her living room. He might even know something about pruning shrubbery.

She pulled herself out of the sheltering cushions of the chaise longue and padded across the porch and onto her lawn.

Grant had pulled a box to the edge of the truck's tailgate and was rummaging through it impatiently. Finally, he lifted something out. From halfway across the lawn, Hayley couldn't distinguish what the object was, but whatever it was, it fit in one hand. He carried it to the far end of the narrow pier that jutted out into the lake and stood there in one of those prolonged moments of motionlessness, facing the water for some time.

She could turn tail and run back to her house, and he'd never know she'd been there, Hayley thought. He was that preoccupied. But, fascinated by the forlorn, solitary figure staring out at the water, Hayley stopped just short of stepping onto the wood planking of the pier.

A patch of thin fog skated over the tip of the pier, fuzzying his silhouette and adding an eery, ethereal touch to the scene. The entire tableau was so like a painting that Hayley was startled into a gasp when, with a sudden violent motion, Grant pitched whatever he had been holding into the lake and shouted, "Sink, you son of a bitch!"

The acoustical trick of a still night and water amplifying his whispering enabled her to hear him add, "Sink all the way to hell—it's where you belong."

He'd disrupted the natural order of the night. The equally sudden unnatural silence that followed the outburst was so profound that neither frog nor cricket nor bird violated it; it caused a shiver to run down Hayley's spine.

She must have made a sound then to breach the extraordinary quiet, because Grant spun round, tense enough to challenge a bear, and looking as though he half expected to have to. He caught sight of Hayley and glared at her for a moment, then barked a word that would have been bleeped on network television.

Hayley felt her face flame. "I'm sorry," she said. "I didn't mean to intrude."

He released a sigh that sounded like a balloon deflating. "You scared the bejesus out of me, lady!"

His harsh, accusatory tone grated on her overwrought nerves. It had just occurred to her to speculate on what hand-size objects a man might throw into a lake with admonitions for it to sink to hell and she didn't like the list of possibilities.

She backed away involuntarily as he advanced toward her. "I'm Hayley Addison, your neighbor," she said.

"I wasn't even sure you were real. This fog—" To Grant, it was as though the fog had taken form in the shape of a curly-haired temptress.

"I saw you drive up. I just wanted to say—" He was staring at her as though he could see through her and suddenly Hayley couldn't remember what she'd wanted to say. She felt exposed, knowing he could read the embarrassment—and the fear—in her eyes easily.

I don't need this! Grant thought wearily. He hadn't wanted any witnesses to his private purging. "So you saw my little ceremony."

She swallowed. "Obviously I've come at a bad time. I'll just—"

She was scared to death, her eyes wide as saucers. Obviously she thought she'd interrupted a sadistic murderer disposing of a smoking gun. The gap between reality and her assumption struck Grant as absurdly funny.

He laughed unexpectedly, and the sound of his laughter echoed diabolically over the water, blending with all those exotic creature sounds that were so alien to Hayley. She shivered again.

Grant sobered and said brusquely, "You can relax, Miss Addison. Your life's not in jeopardy. It wasn't a gun."

"I didn't think—"

"Didn't you?" he demanded, cutting her off. "You should see your face. Like Little Miss Muffet when she encountered the spider."

"Obviously I picked a bad time to say hello. I'll just—" She turned, anxious to get away.

"It was my beeper!" he announced to her retreating back.

Hayley stopped, and slowly pivoted to face him. "Your *beeper?*"

"Until five o'clock this afternoon, I was a slave to that damned hunk of electronic metal and plastic."

The bitterness in his voice confirmed her initial impression that he was a very troubled man. She didn't respond to that bitterness, but replied with studied nonchalance, "I guess anyone who's ever had a beeper has wanted to throw it into a river at one time or another."

He pinned her with an almost-accusatory look. "Precious few ever find the guts to actually do it."

"Precious few can afford to."

"Ah, yes! The almighty dollar!"

"People do have to work for a living."

Grant had been at the end of his patience even before Little Miss Muffet had materialized on the scene. Now his night wraith was spouting platitudes. It was too much for a mortal man. Too much.

"People aren't just working for a living," he informed her. "They're working for the next status symbol, selling their human dignity for the latest toy, selling their souls to companies that don't give a damn about anything but the bottom line."

This speech was received with an extremely uncomfortable silence. Finally, Grant asked, "What about you, Miss Addison—do you have a beeper?"

She shrugged. "I always work at my desk."

"Ah, yes. The accountant. So you subject yourself to computers and calculators instead."

"How did you know—?"

"Mrs. Garth."

"Mrs. Garth. Of course."

Grant affected a falsetto, lockjawed imitation of the real estate agent. "'You'll like the woman who bought the O'Keefes' house, Mr. Mackenzie. Such a lovely girl. An accountant. She transferred down with Hearth Insurance.'"

He cocked an eyebrow. "I'm curious. What did Mrs. Garth have to say about me?"

"Only your name, and that you're a salesman."

"*Was* a salesman," he corrected.

"And now you're an entrepreneur," Hayley said, nodding her head toward the bait shop.

"Don't fancy it up. I'm just a simple worm merchant."

"And I, for one, am very glad of it."

Grant cocked an eyebrow inquiringly, wondering what possible twist of logic would make her care about his avocation.

It was his first display of active interest in the conversation, and Hayley responded to it with a smile before explaining, "Mrs. O'Keefe didn't want to split the property. She never would have agreed to sell me the house if she hadn't had a buyer for the bait shop."

"Mrs. Garth gave me the same story about you and the house."

Hayley wasn't sure, but she thought she heard a note of wry humor in the remark. "It worked out well for both of us," she said.

"And for Mrs. O'Keefe," Grant added. "Not to mention Mrs. Garth, who got a tidy commission on the sales."

"Mrs. Garth said Mrs. O'Keefe was delighted to find a buyer who wanted to reopen the bait shop. Apparently, building it was the realization of her husband's retirement dream, and she was glad his legacy was going to be passed on.

"God!" Grant groaned. He didn't want to be entrusted with the responsibility of a legacy; he was doing his damnedest to rid himself of as much responsibility as he possibly could. So far he'd managed to unload his condo, his luxury sedan and his beeper.

Little Miss Muffet was looking at him expectantly, waiting for him to explain his attitude, and Grant wondered at the perverse fate that had saddled him with a tidy little bundle of temptation when he least needed the irritation of sexual frustration. She was going to be trouble, this curly-haired wraith with the big eyes.

"I bought a bait shop, plain and simple," he said. "I'm going to sell a few worms, a few spinners and flies.

Don't make me responsible for holding up someone's dream."

An awkward silence followed. Wanting to avoid his gaze, Hayley looked out at the lake. The fog had thickened in patches and hovered in thin wisps above the surface of the water.

"The lake's beautiful, isn't it?" she asked, at length.

"It's a lake." He was more impressed with the way the moonlight glinted off her hair—a fact that made him hopping mad at himself.

"It's so . . . tranquil, especially with the fog—Oh, look! In the center, there. A rowboat!"

The small boat was perhaps twenty yards beyond the end of the dock. A solitary boatman slid the oars silently through the water.

"Should we turn on some lights or something, in case he's trying to come ashore?" Hayley asked.

Saints preserve us, she's out to save the world! Grant thought, feeling as though he were standing in shifting sands. "He should be able to see the lights in the shop windows well enough, if he's looking. It's probably a fisherman rowing out to his favorite spot to anchor for the night and get a jump on the predawn fishing."

"In this fog?"

"It's a small lake, and there's no danger of rain or high winds tonight. Even if he should lose his direction in the fog, the worst that could happen is that he'd drift until morning—or float in to shore."

He followed her gaze to the spot where the row boat had been, but the fog had shifted, and where the small boat had been silhouetted by the moonlight, now there was only a thick patch of fog.

"You can't see it anymore," Hayley said with a shiver. "It's as though it was swallowed up by the night."

Damn it, why did she have to shiver like that? It was enough to make a man want to wrap his arms around her. "A bit dramatic, aren't you?" he snapped.

Hayley smiled guiltily. "Just a city girl out of her element." She sighed softly. "It is romantic, isn't it? The mist, and the full moon. I wonder if it was like this the night they eloped."

"Who?" Grant asked absently. Between the sigh and the breathless quality of her voice, he was finding it difficult to concentrate on what she was saying.

Hayley looked at him in surprise. "The man who built my house had a daughter, and she and her boyfriend eloped in a rowboat. That's why they call it Lovers' Lake. Didn't Mrs. Garth tell you the story?"

"We were too busy discussing the development on the far side of the lake to discuss how it got its name."

"The marina complex?" The development included condos, a waterfront restaurant and several boat-launching slips. "Will it cut into your business?"

"Just the opposite," he said. "It should be a boon. There'll be a lot more traffic on the lake. It'll be more convenient for the fishermen to anchor in at my pier for bait than to make a special trip for supplies, especially the ones that live in the condos."

"So you should be able to establish a strong customer base."

He chortled in disdain. "I don't give a damn about 'establishing a customer base,' lady. I'm just going to run a bait shop."

Sacred bastion of macho escapees from the rat race, Hayley thought, but refrained from saying it. Instead she shifted her weight, poised for retreat. "Do you, uh, need a hand moving in, or . . . anything? I could make a pot of coffee."

"What? You didn't bring a cake?" It wouldn't surprise him if she had. She was the type.

"Do they really still do that in the South?"

"Relax, Miss Addison. I was just being sarcastic. I assure you, I've moved a number of times, and I've never once had a neighbor bring me cake."

Not surprising, if you're always so full of cheer, Hayley thought. "Since we seem to know each other well enough for sarcasm," she said, "and since we *are* going to be living next door to each other, why don't you call me Hayley?"

"Hayley. The accountant."

She stiffened at his mocking, disdainful tone. "That's right."

He shrugged away her annoyance. "Call me Grant."

"Grant. The worm merchant," she returned sharply.

So Little Miss Muffet isn't all romantic whimsy and neighborly charm. "You got it."

"I'll try to remember it."

Grant let her get halfway to her house before calling, "Hayley?"

She turned.

"Next time, bring cake. I'll make tea. We'll have a tea party."

A shake of her head was her only reply. *When hell freezes over, I'll bring you an ice-cream cake, Mr. Grant Mackenzie, worm merchant!*

2

GRANT WATCHED HIS NEW neighbor lug plastic bags distended by vegetables, milk cartons and canned goods from her car to her house. *So Little Miss Muffet had been grocery shopping.*

He could, he supposed, dash out and offer to help. There was a time when he would have. *Good old Grant Mackenzie. Always courteous. Ever the gentleman and charmer.*

Today, the new Grant quelled the impulse. If he carried Miss Muffet's groceries inside for her, he'd just end up talking to her again; and getting chummy with his new neighbor was the last thing he wanted or needed. He hadn't quit his job, leased out his condo, traded his luxury sedan for a used pickup and moved into the back room of a bait shop so that he could get tangled up with a woman like Hayley Addison. He was severing ties, not seeking new ones. He was the new, reformed Grant: no strings, no responsibility, no pressure, no expectations, no disappointments. *No big-eyed, gamine women who were brimming over with expectations.*

Poor Miss Muffet. She had expectation written all over her. She'd talked about that couple eloping on the lake as though she'd witnessed it—she probably believed, way down inside, that someday a man would row up to whisk her away in the moonlight.

And responsibility. She was one of those people who flourished under the weight of responsibility. She was mired up to her alluring little neck in it. A job as a corporate accountant. A house, complete with mortgage. Mrs. Garth had even mentioned that Hayley was studying for the CPA exam.

Let Hayley Addison, future CPA, carry in her own damn groceries! She represented everything he was leaving behind. He had enough to do getting the bait shop open. All morning he'd cleaned and sorted, and now he was sifting though O'Keefe's telephone files. Despite the quaintness of his system—a metal recipe can filled with three-by-five-inch cards—O'Keefe had been thorough. The cards were filed alphabetically by name, with addresses, telephone numbers and dated notations.

There were suppliers for worms, crickets, shiners, flies and lures, periodicals and sundry food items. On Monday, Grant would begin calling them. And he'd get in touch with O'Keefe's contact at the Fish and Game Commission to see what was involved with selling fishing licenses. Now, he planned to skim through the old-fashioned cloth-bound ledgers in which O'Keefe had methodically recorded his weekly supply purchases to get a handle on the quantities he should order.

Later, he was going to go out and buy himself a decent bed. Giving up a posh condominium and all its

trappings for the back room of a bait shop was a statement; sleeping on the army-surplus cot O'Keefe had left
there was just plain stupid. A man owed his back
something. A single bed with a good solid mattress
shouldn't compromise the integrity of his rejection of
his old value system, as long as he didn't dress it up with
designer sheets and comforters. He was downgrading,
after all, from king-size.

He would also, he supposed, have to pick up a few
groceries—enough to throw together an occasional
sandwich.

First things first, he thought as he sat down at the
desk behind the counter and opened the ledgers.

He was totally absorbed in the records when he heard
footsteps on the porch. A quick glance out the window
told him who his visitor was: Little Miss Muffet, back
like a boomerang. Or like the headache from a hang-
over. He pushed the ledger aside and waited for her
knock.

"We're not open for business yet," he called. "Come
back in two weeks."

Hayley was sorely tempted to turn around and leave.
Obviously Grant Mackenzie was as obnoxious by light
of day as he'd been in the dark of night. "It's not a customer," she said. "It's Hayley. From next door."

"Did you bring me a cake?"

"I brought you some mail." *If it had been anything
less official than mail, I wouldn't have bothered, you
arrogant turkey!*

"Door's not locked."

Southern hospitality in action, Hayley thought, giving the doorknob a savage twist. She noted that at least Grant had the grace to rise as she entered the room. Without preamble, she slapped a manila envelope on the counter. "This was in my box. I didn't realize it was for you until I was going through my mail."

Grant glowered at the envelope as though loath to touch it. Hayley could literally see the tension in his body as he examined the logo on the mailing label. Her initial impression had been accurate: Grant Mackenzie was a very troubled man.

A wave of compassion made her want to reach out to him with a reassuring touch, perhaps to test his day-old beard with her fingertips. His beard was tawny and golden, like his hair, and appeared downy soft where it shadowed his cheeks.

Deciding that he'd only resent it if she tried to help, she said crossly, "There's only one mailbox. The O'Keefes must have gotten their personal mail and the mail for the shop in the same box."

"So now I need a separate mailbox for the shop, is that it?"

"If you catch the mailman when he's making his rounds, he should be able to tell you the proper procedure for putting up another one."

"I'll take care of it."

"In the interim, I'll check the mail before I open it and bring you any mail you get."

He shrugged. "If it's not too much trouble."

"It's not." *Yes, it is!* she thought. *It's going to be a big inconvenience, but I don't want you looking at my mail.* She wasn't sure why the idea of his seeing her mail bothered her. What was there to see, anyway? The outside of sealed envelopes. The white linen stationery her mother always used? The unicorn-festooned postalettes her niece sealed with moon-shaped stickers? Her utility bill and the monthly statement from her only credit card? It wasn't as though she got X-rated postcards from mysterious lovers.

That was it. She didn't particularly want mysterious lovers sending her X-rated postcards, but she wasn't any more comfortable with Grant Mackenzie knowing that there were no lovers in her life. It was too personal. *Too revealing.*

"I shouldn't be getting much mail," he said.

Hayley wanted to leave, but didn't know how to do so graciously. To avoid looking at him, she pretended interest in a jumble of lures stacked in a small box on the counter, and picked one up. The maroon-and-yellow body resembled a miniature banana and wore what appeared to be a skirt of plastic fringe. As she lifted it, one of the wicked-looking multipronged hooks protruding from the plastic skirt caught on another lure. She shook it gently, trying to free it.

"Careful," Grant warned. "Those are—"

"Ow!" Hayley dropped the lure and raised her thumb to her mouth.

"Sharp," Grant finished irritably. "Let's see."

Hayley jerked her hand away as he reached for it. "It's just a prick."

"Let's see," Grant persisted.

Grudgingly, Hayley let him cradle her hand and turn her thumb toward the window to examine it in the sunlight. He was surprisingly gentle, and his concern seemed genuine.

Gentle and caring. It was a new side of Grant, but Hayley wasn't ready to drop her defenses and like him at one fleeting display of human sensitivity.

And fleeting it was. "You're right," he said, releasing her hand with an air of dismissal. "Just a prick."

Hayley flashed him an I-told-you-so scowl.

"You were lucky. The point got you, but the hook didn't go in far enough for the barb to engage. It could have been very messy."

He was right, of course. But he didn't have to make her feel like a careless child. Hayley released an exaggerated sigh. "I might have *bled* all over your floor!"

"Digging it out would have hurt like hell."

"*You* wouldn't have felt a thing," she said, glaring at him.

Wondering what he'd done to ruffle her feathers, Grant glared back. A man had to worry about a full-grown woman with no more sense than to stick a fishhook in her thumb.

Oh, no, you don't! he told himself. *You don't have to worry about anybody, particularly a* woman *with no better sense than to stick a fishhook in her thumb!*

No matter how big her eyes are or how soft her skin is.

Even in the brief seconds he'd held her hand, he'd noticed the softness of her skin. And he'd noticed much more that.

Like the way she smelled—all wildflowers and fresh air—and the way her hair curled around her face. All of which reminded him how very long it had been since he'd touched a woman who was soft and had curly hair and smelled like wildflowers.

Forever, he thought. At least, it seemed like forever. And that's how long it would be before he touched Hayley Addison again. Because he didn't want to worry about another living soul, and because she was the type who could make him worry about her because she didn't have sense enough not to stick a fishhook in her thumb. And because all he wanted was a comfortable little life running a bait shop, and Hayley Addison was studying for the CPA examination.

And because if he touched her again, he'd be tempted to hold more than her hand. He was already tempted.

"I've got to go," she said.

"So soon?"

"I'm—" She hesitated, trying to make up something that would sound credible. "Expecting a phone call."

Outside, a boat engine idled, then stopped. They heard the creak and groan of a boat rubbing against the tires hung along the sides of the dock. Hayley and Grant looked out the window and saw a white-haired man tying the docking line of his boat to a post.

He finished his knot and, as though sensing his audience, turned and waved. He gestured again, and a dog, a hound of some sort, leaped out of the boat and fell into step beside his master.

"Howdy," the boatman said, as he entered, with the dog still at his heels.

"Hello," Hayley replied, and noticed that Grant merely nodded.

"Master Sergeant Edward Drews, U.S. Army, retired," the man said, stretching a long arm to extend his hand to Grant. "Everyone nowadays calls me Slim. I live just around the bend. I heard someone had bought O'Keefe's store, and thought I'd putter over and say hello."

Grant, shaking Slim's hand, introduced himself.

"Good to meet you, Grant," said Slim. He nodded at Hayley. "You, too, Mrs. Mackenzie."

Hayley was sorely tempted to say something quite rude, but responded, "Actually, it's Addison."

"*Miss* Addison," Grant added smugly.

"Hayley," she corrected, ignoring Grant, who was enjoying her embarrassment far too much. "I bought the O'Keefes' house."

Slim pumped her hand with the grip and enthusiasm of a born politician. "Nice to meet you, Hayley."

"Does your dog bite?" she asked.

Slim chortled. "Penrod? Hell, no—excuse the French ma'am. Penrod might drown you in drool if you make a fuss over him, but I've never seen him bite into anything that wasn't edible."

Grant thought, as Hayley knelt to pet the dog, that whether or not Hayley Addison could be considered edible was debatable. There were moments when he was all too aware of how delectable he found her.

Moments of madness, he thought sourly.

Penrod threw his head back and closed his eyes in an expression of almost obscene ecstasy as Hayley stroked his neck.

"Smartest dog I ever had," Slim remarked, looking at Grant with a knowing expression that made Grant worry that his wayward thoughts might not be too far from the surface.

"He's adorable," Hayley said, oblivious to the masculine exchange between the two men.

"You wouldn't want one sorta like him, would you? Old Penrod here dug under the fence and knocked up the neighbor's prize bloodhound bitch. I'm not talking ugly, ma'am—that's what they call female dogs."

"I know," Hayley replied.

Slim laughed. "George—that's my neighbor, the one who owns the bloodhound—bred her with another bloodhound last year and she only produced two pups. George sold them for seven hundred bucks each. Penrod here sired eight, and they aren't worth a plug nickel without papers. George is fit to be tied. I told him it just goes to prove that highfalutin' papers don't prove nothing when it comes to shootin' straight."

Hayley tilted her head back to look at Slim. "I've been thinking about getting a puppy. For company."

"The mama dog's weaning 'em now, if you want one," Slim offered.

A puppy! Grant thought. He might have known. The woman soaked up responsibility like a sponge. She *yearned* for it.

"Puppies yip all night and wet all over everything," he said sourly.

"Only at first," Hayley corrected, flashing him an exasperated, mind-your-own-business scowl before turning a more benign expression on Slim. "The problem is, I work all day. Do you think a puppy would get too lonely?"

Slim shook his head. "Naw. You've got a yard. Put up a run for him, and give him some toys, he'll be just fine."

"A run?"

"Some fencing. Hell, Penrod's getting on in years. I wouldn't mind having one of his pups close enough to catch a glimpse of every now and then. You buy the fencing, I'll put it up for you."

"That's an offer I can't refuse."

"You're going to make George's day," Slim said with a chuckle. "If you're not busy, we could boat on over there and you can pick out your pup."

"I'm not—" she began, then stopped midsentence and looked at Grant to see if he'd noticed her slip. He had. Oh, yes, he'd noticed. He was biting back a grin and enjoying her guilt to the hilt. She thrust her chin up defiantly, and told Slim, "I'm not busy. I'd love to go pick out a puppy."

"Weren't you expecting a phone call?" Grant asked, feigning so much innocence that Hayley could almost believe he was showing signs of a sense of humor.

"My machine's on," she said. "They'll leave a message."

Grant crossed his arms over his waist and hitched his hip against the counter. Her machine was on. Naturally, she'd have a machine. He'd left his at the condo—one more amenity for the lessee—and he was glad of it. Good riddance. He didn't need machines to speak for him or to listen for him anymore.

Slim, seemingly oblivious to the tension between Hayley and Grant, surveyed the room curiously. "You getting ready to start reshelving everything?"

"As soon as I've had a chance to go through it."

"If you need any help, I'm available. I know where everything used to go. I used to fill in for O'Keefe when he wanted a few hours off. Then when I took a hankering to go fishing, I didn't have to worry about bait."

"I'll remember your offer," Grant said. He liked the concept of bartering time for bait. It was the type of simplicity and male practicality that had prompted his choosing a bait shop. "I'm going to start ordering at the first of the week and I'll stock as merchandise comes in."

"Sure hope you get Moon Pie sandwiches. Nothing tastes better when you're out on the water than cold beer and a Moon Pie."

"I'll order some."

"You order 'em, and I'll eat 'em," Slim said. "Well, Hayley, you ready to go get yourself a dog?"

"Sure am!" Hayley exclaimed.

"Why don't you go along with us, Grant?" Slim invited. "It'll give you a chance to see the lake. I can show you my place on the way."

"No, thanks," Grant said. "I have to make some kind of sense out of these ledgers."

"Well, guess we'll see you later, then," Slim said, gallantly cupping Hayley's elbow to guide her from the shop.

His boat was a modest craft that showed the rigors of age; the bait buckets, ice chest and tackle boxes were sun-faded and scratched from long use. "It's not fancy, but it gets me to the fish," Slim explained, without apology. He took the chair behind the wheel and Penrod, apparently from long habit, leaped onto the chair next to his master's and braced his front paws against the dashboard.

Slim looked at his dog, then over his shoulder at Hayley. "Sorry about Penrod's manners. He sits in that chair so often he thinks he has squatter's rights to it. Just take one of the seats along either side."

The engine hummed like an energetic bumblebee as it churned up the water behind them. Hayley closed her eyes, tilted her head back to catch the sun, and sighed.

From inside the bait shop, Grant watched the boat until it slid out of sight around the bend noting, with much displeasure, Hayley Addison's alluringly displayed neck and the way her hair danced in the breeze.

Her legs weren't bad, either. Mumbling a curse under his breath, he stuck his nose back in the ledger and tried to concentrate.

In the boat, Slim took his role as host and tour guide seriously and provided a running commentary on the lake and its landmarks as they followed the shoreline.

"Do you know anything about the couple who eloped?" Hayley asked, during a lull in the narrative. "The ones who gave the lake its name?"

"Not much," Slim replied. "That was back just after the war. World War II. Old Arthur Ramsey—he was the man who built your house—had a daughter, and I guess he kept her pretty much locked away from everything. Anyway, she met a man and fell in love, but Old Ramsey didn't approve. The story is that when he forbade her to see him, her lover rowed in to get her."

"That's very romantic."

"For the couple involved, I suppose," Slim said. "It drove Old Man Ramsey crazy. Word is, he raised all manner of hell at first, demanded that the law find her and bring her back, but she was above the age of consent. Ramsey just couldn't accept that she would defy him and leave like that. He slowly went nuts thinking about it. Lived off the land. Let his hair and beard grow like a madman's."

"Did you know him?"

"Just from a distance. Got too close to shore once when I first moved here and found myself on the receiving end of his shotgun. Still got some pockmarks on the side of the boat to show for it. He used to shoot at anybody who got too close to his property, including the authorities."

"They didn't arrest him?"

"Just warned him. He was an excellent shot. The law figured if he'd wanted to hurt anybody, he would have. Since he didn't, they figured it was best to leave him alone. People just made a wide berth around his place."

"This is the man who used to sleep in my house," Hayley observed.

Slim laughed. "I wouldn't worry too much about that. If he left any bad vibrations behind, I'm sure Agnes O'Keefe sent them flying out the window. She and O'Keefe redid that house from top to bottom. Paint, wallpaper, windows, central air, refinished woodwork, new appliances in the kitchen. They're the ones who added the Florida room. O'Keefe said his wife loved decorating and fixing up, and he was glad to let her at it, because it kept her busy while he was building the bait shop and pier."

"How did he die?" Hayley asked.

"Old Man Ramsey, or O'Keefe?"

"Ramsey."

"Natural causes. Old age, mostly. They found him near that clump of gardenia bushes after boaters reported seeing a body there."

"How awful!" Hayley shivered. "Gardenias. Is that what those trees in the center of the backyard are? The ones with the shiny leaves?"

"Those are the ones," Slim said. "But, technically, they're shrubs, not trees."

"They're covered with buds. I wondered what the flowers would look like."

"White. In another week or two, they'll be covered." He shook his head. "If Ramsey had died inside when those damned gardenias were in bloom, no one would have found him. The smell of gardenias would mask a rotting elephant. Don't know why in the world a man would plant a mess of gardenia shrubs like that, so close together. Of course, they're pretty when they're blooming, but the smell'll knock you over. I catch whiffs of them all the way over at my place when the wind is right."

Slim chuckled. "O'Keefe hated them. Claimed they gave him hay fever. But he kept them, because Agnes liked them. Don't know why. You can't do much with them. The petals bruise and turn brown if they're touched, and they don't have a stalk, so the only way to decorate with them is to float them in water. The society crowd used to put them in swimming pools, but I haven't heard of anyone doing that lately. Not that I travel in that crowd."

He cut the motor to an idle. "Here we are. This is my dock. We'll cut through my yard to get to George's."

As Slim had predicted, George, a potbellied man with hairy legs, was overjoyed at the prospect of unloading one of the puppies to a good home. He immediately took his visitors to the Florida room, where the mother dog lay surrounded by her frolicking offspring. George stroked the bloodhound's head, reassuring her, while Hayley knelt to study the puppies. She wanted them all, every single one of those wrinkled, spotted little mongrels: the curious one, who came sniffing up to smell her; the clumsy one, who kept tripping over his own oversize feet; the cautious one, who stayed close enough to touch his mother and eyed Hayley surreptitiously; the bold one, who growled at her; the runt, smaller than all the others but determined to keep up with his larger siblings; the feisty one, who barked at her with a voice that showed promise of a bloodhound yodel; and the twins, who looked exactly alike down to the kinks in their tails, and rough-and-tumbled together in a mock dogfight.

Hayley picked up each one in turn, examined and hugged it. Still cradling the runt in her lap, she looked up at Slim. "How am I supposed to choose? They're all sweet."

"Why don't you let one choose you," Slim suggested. "Have a seat and see which one refuses to be ignored."

The suggestion made sense, so Hayley sat down on a wicker chair and watched the puppies. One of them was trying to nurse and being roundly discouraged by its mother. Two, including the runt, had curled up and fallen asleep, and the other five were playing, tumbling around and growling at each other. The feisty one, the loudest growler of the bunch, seemed suddenly to tire of the game. He sat down, threw his head back and sniffed the air, then jumped up and began tracking a scent across the patio floor. After several serpentine detours, he traced Hayley's path to the love seat and, after sniffing her feet, took a step backward and barked that baying, bloodhound bark.

"Well, Hayley?" Slim asked, chuckling.

"That's a male," George said.

The puppy barked again. He was so filled with bluster and self-importance, and yet so tiny, that Hayley couldn't resist. She bent over and picked up the baying little bag of wrinkled, spotted fur.

Even as she held it in her lap, the puppy barked at her until, laughing, she calmed it by scratching it behind the ears. The bloodhound bay became a satisfied whimper as the pup responded to Hayley's attention.

"No doubt about it," Slim said. "You've got yourself a dog."

The puppy was the sole topic of conversation on the ride back to the bait shop. Grant came out to the pier in time to tie the stern line while Slim held on to one of the tires to keep the bow from drifting.

"There's no reason for me to get out," Slim said. "You can help Hayley out, can't you, Grant?"

Grant nodded. "Sure."

Hayley thanked Slim for taking her to get the puppy and gingerly crossed the width of the boat. She tucked the puppy under her left arm and reached for Grant's outstretched hand. It was not a big step to the dock, but each time she shifted her weight to prepare for the maneuver, the boat bobbed. After several futile tries, she laughed nervously. "I'm not used to boats."

"You need an arm to balance," Grant said gruffly. "Give me the puppy." His impatience irritated Hayley.

Talk about a grouch! It wasn't as though she'd been around boats all her life.

Hayley held the puppy out to him. "Be gentle. He's little."

As if I go around abusing small dogs, Grant thought, as he eased the puppy from her hands. Cradling it against his chest with his right hand, he extended his left to Hayley again. "Now, lead with your right leg and just jump."

Hayley turned to tell Slim goodbye again before gripping Grant's hand, counting to three and jumping.

Working one-handedly, Grant untied the stern rope and tossed it back into the boat, and waved as Slim took off. Then, suddenly, he cursed.

Hayley turned to him in surprise.

He held the puppy out to her, holding it by the scruff of the neck. "You can have your dog back," he snarled. She took it, murmuring endearments as she cuddled it. Then she noticed the large wet spot on the front of Grant's shirt.

"Sorry about that," she said lamely.

The apology did nothing to soften the scowl on Grant's face.

Irked by his attitude, Hayley snapped, "Well, he's just a baby. You probably made him nervous." Then she stalked off with the puppy securely cradled between her breasts.

3

"OUCH!"

The sharp hook had penetrated the skin of her index finger. Hayley raised her finger to her mouth.

"Let me see."

Grant, looking very James Bondish in a black tuxedo, reached for her hand. Hayley looked down at her clothes. She was dressed as formally, in an off-the-shoulder black silk that clung to her breasts and hugged her waist, then billowed into a full skirt.

He guided her hand to his lips and kissed her wounded finger; then, still holding her hand, he looked at her across her fingertips. His gaze was warm, smoldering with sensuality. He stared at her lips, and she opened them slightly and moistened them with her tongue, issuing an invitation.

He kissed her fingertips, one by one, unhurriedly. She gasped as he nipped at her thumb, then sucked on it gently. The gasp became a prolonged sigh as he kissed his way down her thumb to her palm, her wrist, then up her arm to her shoulders.

By the time his mouth covered hers, every muscle in her body was tensed in anticipation of that first taste. She parted her lips and returned the kiss hungrily, *wrapped her arms around him to pull him close, and greedily explored his back with her hands.*

Suddenly she was being carried into a huge room with high ceilings and intricate wainscoting. The only light came from a roaring fire in a massive fireplace.

Carefully, Grant lowered her in front of the inferno and stretched out with her. His body pressed hers into the thick fur of the rug. The fur tickled her bare shoulders as he kissed her, but it was the places he touched that were inflamed. She kissed him with wanton abandon.

He removed her shoe, with its scandalously high, sinfully-pointed stiletto heel, and tossed it away with a spate of wicked laughter. The heat of his fingers burned through her silk stockings as he followed their sheerness from ankle to calf to knee, and then singed the bare skin of her thigh as he deftly undid the garters of her lace-and-satin garter belt. After peeling her stockings off, he rained a trail of kisses along the same path, from her ankle to her knee and higher....

She moaned and urged him on. "Kiss me, Grant. Yes. Oh, yes. Don't stop—"

"Tramp!"

The voice was a gruff roar, the word a condemnation. Hayley opened her eyes. Grant had gone, evaporated into the darkness of her bedroom, but her body still tingled with the memory of intimate caresses, still cried out for fulfillment. At the foot of the bed, her accuser stood, glaring at her; his gray straggly hair and beard seemed to glow in the dim light.

"Tramp! Slut! Harlot! You let him degrade you and lead you into iniquity."

Hayley pushed up on her elbows and shook her head to clear it—and watch her accuser fade into the shadows of the still unfamiliar room. She stared stupidly at the now empty space, then, with a bewildered sigh, sank back into her pillows.

It was a dream. But it had been so real. That horrid old man, shouting accusations like a character out of *The Scarlet Letter*, must have been Arthur Ramsey. Jeez! Was she susceptible to suggestion, or what?

And Grant making love to her on a fur rug. Grant Mackenzie of all people! He was the last person in the world she should be fantasizing about, asleep or awake. She didn't like the man, and from all indications, the antipathy was mutual. So why did her subconscious zero in on him for an X-rated scenario in her sleep?

That awful Ramsey character, calling her names, couldn't have been as weird on his worst day as her mind had painted him. *Lead her into iniquity?* Hayley rolled over and groaned into her pillow. If the real Arthur Ramsey was like the one in her dream, it was no wonder his daughter had rowed off into the night with her lover.

Her restless shifting had awakened the puppy. She tried to ignore the tiny paws scratching against cardboard walls, but the puppy's yowl was not to be ignored.

"All right. All right!" she said finally, tossing the covers back. She knelt next to the cardboard box where

the puppy had been put to bed with a ticking clock and
a soft old towel and lifted the puppy out. "You know it's
four-thirty in the morning, don't you?" She yawned.
"It's a good thing tomorrow's Sunday so I can sleep in."

Half an hour later it was apparent she wasn't going
to get any sleep until her new pet had worked off some
of the youthful energy that had been restored by his
long nap. She played with him until she nodded off
while seated in the middle of the floor, then jerked
awake as she pitched sideways.

Hayley scooped the pupping into her hands. "This is
ridiculous," she said. "It's back in the box for you, and
back to bed for me."

The puppy had other ideas. Finally, after what
seemed hours of his leaping and baying, Hayley sur-
rendered to the inevitable and lifted the puppy onto the
bed. "You're missing your mama and brothers and sis-
ters, aren't you?" she asked groggily as she cuddled the
puppy against her midriff. "Well, I miss my family,
too."

The puppy yawned, propped his chin on Hayley's
arm and drifted off to sleep. Half-asleep, Hayley murmured, "No offense, little guy, but this wasn't exactly
what I was dreaming about."

Her last muddled thought as she dozed off was that
if Arthur Ramsey had felt compelled to invade her
dreams and call her names, he could at least have
waited until the good parts were over.

GRANT HEARD THE SOUND again—a guttural whimper of distress. This time, he put aside the catalog and the order form he'd been filling out. He was past due for a break. Maybe if he took a walk, he could track down the plaintive cry.

He paused on the porch to try to pinpoint the direction from which the sound was coming. Listening intently, he traced it to the clump of gardenia bushes in Hayley's yard. Warily, he pushed aside the branches of one of the shrubs, hoping he wasn't on the verge of an encounter with a wounded bobcat—or worse.

Catching sight of the source of all the commotion, he groaned in exasperation. "I might have known!"

He gripped the puppy by the scruff of the neck and lifted him out of the jungle of limbs. "How'd you get in there in the first place?"

The dog yelped and squirmed so fiercely that Grant was forced to cradle him in his arms to hold on to him. The puppy calmed instantly, and began licking Grant's arm. "Yeah, yeah, yeah," Grant said. "Well, I would have done the same for any animal in trouble. Let's see where you're *supposed* to be. I can't believe Little Miss Muffet would let you roam free."

He put the pup down, and it followed him, running to keep up with his long strides. Grant stopped a few feet short of Hayley's house. The bottom corner of one of the screen panels on the Florida room had been pushed through. "Well, it doesn't take Sherlock Holmes to solve this case," Grant told the dog. "You made a jailbreak, didn't you, boy?"

The doors to the porch were locked, so Grant was forced to return the puppy to the Florida room through the same hole the little stinker had used to escape. The porch, Grant noted, was cluttered with evidence of a well-cared-for pet: food and water dishes, play balls, leather chew bones, newspapers.

The puppy sniffed his way across the floor until he encountered one of his chew bones and, after giving it a thorough smelling, picked it up and began chomping on it. Grant felt comfortable leaving him there long enough to go after duct tape to repair the screen. Halfway back to the bait shop, he heard the puppy yodel, and by the time he'd found the tape and started back to Hayley's porch, the little guy was crossing the lawn, following Grant's scent with the intense concentration of one of his ancestors on the trail of an escaped convict. He turned as Grant passed him and followed Grant back to the porch.

Grant picked him up and held him at eye level. "Look, you little rapscallion, this is Hayley's house, and you're Hayley's dog. This is where you belong."

With this logical appeal, he gingerly returned the pup to the porch and applied duct tape to the torn screening. "That ought to hold you."

The pup barked and yelped, but Grant paid no heed. He'd done his good deed for the day. He'd get himself a dog if he wanted the hassle of a dog. He didn't.

The barking wasn't so easy to ignore when the puppy was on the bait-shop porch. Grant opened the door and, with his hands planted on his waist in stern disapproval, looked down at the determined little dog. The puppy was not in the least intimidated, but dashed forward to lick Grant's ankles in welcome, wagging his tail with such fervor that his entire body swayed with the motion.

"Oh, no, you don't," Grant said. "Don't try buttering me up. You're going back to where you belong. We discussed that, didn't we?"

The dog followed Grant obligingly. Once again, Grant deposited him on the porch, then applied another row of duct tape to the screen. "This much tape would stymie Houdini," he told the dog through the screen.

He was not as unaffected by the puppy's whimpering and barking as he would have liked, but he made it back to the bait shop without a backward glance.

The dog was scratching at the bait-shop door within minutes. This time, Grant opened the door and, once the dog was inside, closed it. "You may as well stay. Little Miss Muffet would never forgive me if I let you get lost."

The puppy braced his front paws on Grant's legs just below the knee and barked. "Don't get any ideas," Grant told him. "This is a short-term arrangement. You've got a mistress who obviously takes very good care of you."

Determined to finish what the dog had interrupted, Grant returned to his desk and the catalogs and inventory lists. The half bloodhound explored the bait shop, moving in serpentine forays around the floor.

"You're going to get your nose full of dust," Grant warned, but the tiny dog kept up his explorations, stopping periodically to sniff at anything that attracted his attention. At length he came to Grant and, after giving his worn joggers a thorough going-over, braced his front paws against Grant's thighs and barked.

Grant frowned at the dog; the dog barked again, then added a jump and a hopeful whimper.

"You're used to being held, aren't you? I should have known she'd spoil you rotten."

The puppy gave another jump, another whimper.

"I'm not going to get any peace until I pick you up, am I?" With a sigh of resignation, he helped the puppy into his lap. The dog made a circle on Grant's thighs until he found a comfortable position, then yawned as Grant scratched him behind the ears.

"Just don't think we're going to make a habit of this," Grant grumbled.

SOMETHING WAS WRONG. Bluster always barked to greet her when she got out of the car. Alarmed, Hayley ran to the Florida room. It was empty. Her heart was already in her throat when she spied the silver duct tape and the damaged screen, which despite the repair attempt, was gaping open.

Poor Bluster. Alone and lost. He was so little. He'd be so helpless in the wild. She took a deep breath to calm herself. Think! What should she do?

Someone had tried to repair the screen. There were only two people she could think of who might have been concerned enough to try to repair the screen. Of the two, her money was on Slim. He must have been passing by and had seen or heard Bluster.

And repaired the screen and then left, confident that the puppy was safe and secure.... And then Bluster had escaped again.

Grant's truck was there, so he was probably in the shop. He might have talked to Slim. And he might help her look for Bluster. Surely he wouldn't be cold-hearted enough to a puppy that he would refuse.

Hayley called out to Grant as she neared the bait shop. A familiar blustery, baying bark from inside the shop answered her, and she broke into a run. Just as she reached the porch steps, the shop door opened, and Bluster dashed out to greet her, wagging his tail so fast that he couldn't walk straight. Hayley felt the sting of tears as she scooped him into her arms. She hugged the puppy fiercely, then looked up at Grant, who was standing in the doorway with an expression of wry amusement on his face.

"It's hard to say which of you is happier to see the other."

"I was scared to death," Hayley said. "I came home and he didn't bark or anything, and he was gone, and I saw the screen—" Her eyes narrowed. "Was it you who tried to fix it?"

Grant nodded. "I found him stranded in the gardenias, and took him home, but—"

"Thank you."

Grant had never heard so much emotion packed into two simple words. And her eyes—heaven help him, they were limpid with gratitude. He wanted nothing more at that moment than to take her into his arms and hold her until she was no longer trembling with relief—until she trembled instead from the very closeness of him.

Hayley was recovered enough from her panic over Bluster to recognize the sexual gleam that had appeared in Grant's eyes—and respond to it out of all proportion, as the more erotic details of her dream suddenly came back to her, clear as memories of actual events.

Bluster barked, and she gratefully lowered her head, glad of the diversion, hoping Grant hadn't already seen too much.

"No, Bluster. Calm down! Don't lick!" *That wasn't what you said to Grant in your dream, was it?* she thought, and her face grew warm.

A long moment passed before she risked looking at Grant again, and there was another prolonged moment of awkward silence before she could think of anything to say.

"Your shirt wasn't stained, was it?"

"My shirt?"

"Saturday. When Bluster—"

"It was an old shirt."

"If it was stained, I'll be happy to replace it."

"It wasn't stained."

Another silence ensued before Hayley said, "What you did today—"

"You named him, huh?"

"Huh?"

"The puppy. You gave him a name."

Hayley nodded. "Bluster. It . . . seemed to fit. He's so full of—"

"Piss and vinegar," Grant finished wryly.

"And bluster. I mean, he acts so ferocious, but he's really a big baby. See what I mean?" She bobbed her chin toward Bluster, who had snuggled down in her arms and was resting his chin on the crook of her elbow. "Anyway, thanks again for rescuing him."

Grant shrugged away her gratitude without comment. He didn't want any medals of heroism pinned on his chest. He could hardly have let the little guy roam free. But then, she obviously thought he was the type to send helpless puppies out into the woods alone. She probably thought he drowned kittens for recreation.

She sighed resolutely. "I'd better get this little truant home. I guess it's the laundry room for him until we get the dog run up."

The softness of her sigh evoked erotic images in his mind. "Too bad," he said. It was too bad about more than the dog's plight, he thought, as he watched her walk back to her house. She looked good in narrow skirts, sheer stockings and high-heeled pumps—*too* good.

Hayley was delighted to trade her office clothes for jeans and loafers so she could get down on the floor and rough-and-tumble with Bluster. After a rambunctious session of tug-of-war with one of her old bunny slippers—Bluster's favorite toy—she stretched out on the floor. Bluster climbed onto her chest and licked her chin, still wanting to play.

"Stop that! No licking. No!" Laughing, Hayley caught his muzzle in her hands and looked at him eyeball-to-eyeball. "I was right about you, you know. You *are* good company." Putting him back on the floor, she got up. "I'm starving. Come on into the kitchen. You can sniff all the exotic scents on the floor. I might even share my dinner with you."

Later, she took the puppy outside for a run before nightfall. Since she was judiciously avoiding Grant— had been since the wet-shirt episode on Saturday—they went out the front door. Bluster, as always, set out to discover who and what had been in the yard since the last time he'd been there. "You're wasting your time!" Hayley said. "The only escaped convict around here is *you*, you little—"

Bluster froze suddenly then lifted his nose in the air, sniffing and baying, before he dashed off toward the backyard. Hayley followed on the run, calling him, but didn't catch up with him until he'd reached the dock, where he danced around Grant's feet, barking and wagging his tail as though certain Grant would be delighted to see him.

"I'm sorry," she told Grant. "He just took off. I think he caught your scent."

Grant didn't seem to mind the invasion of his privacy. In fact, he knelt and petted Bluster as though glad to see him. The breeze had lost the heat of the day and was refreshingly cool. Hayley took a deep breath and exhaled it slowly. The setting sun hung like a giant fireball over the western horizon, and the surface of the water caught its golden light.

"It's nice here this time of day," she said.

"Always is," Grant replied. "Most people don't stop long enough to notice."

"Not everyone has a lake. Or a pier."

He patted the planking next to where he'd just sat down. "You can sit on my pier."

Surprise registered on Hayley's face. Had he been that forbidding? he wondered, and smiled tentatively. "The best is yet to come."

"If you're sure—"

"No charge for the parking space or the show."

"Show?"

He pointed to the sun. "It gets even more spectacular."

Already the horizon was aglow with color—orange, red and rose pink that stood out in dramatic contrast to the brilliant blue sky, and the panorama was reflected in the water.

"Do you watch every night?" Hayley asked.

Her voice was soft, soothing. Grant hadn't foreseen that he would miss the sound of other human voices. "I do now."

"But you haven't always?"

His gaze locked with hers. "I never used to slow down long enough."

Hayley wanted to ask about the reasons he'd changed, but instinct made her bite back the question. He was more approachable tonight than he'd ever been before, and she didn't want to risk shattering the tenuous rapport developing between them. Instead, she looked at Bluster, who'd fallen asleep with his chin resting on Grant's thigh. "I think he likes you," she said.

He was absently stroking the puppy, caressing one of the little hound's long ears with his fingertips. "We got acquainted this afternoon."

There was a silence—comfortable, mellow, rich with the romance of the moment. The reflective surface of the lake seemed to swallow up the sun as it sank; the water glowed with the pink halo of light the sun left behind on the horizon.

Gradually, as day shifted into night, the nocturnal sounds seeped into the silence. Hayley tilted her head to listen more closely. "It sounds like an orchestra," she said.

Grant chortled in surprise. "An orchestra of crickets?"

"I've never heard so many all at once." Her laughter was as soft as the night. "It's a funny image, isn't it? Hundreds, thousands of little crickets in tuxedos, playing violins—like in *The Cricket in Times Square*."

"I think you've got a bad case of moon fever."

"Is that terminal?"

"It can be dangerous," Grant answered gravely, the frivolity gone. When a man looked into eyes like Hayley Addison's, moon fever was decidedly dangerous.

"What's that?" The sound had been flatter, less resonant than the chirping.

"A frog."

"Sounds like a Bronx cheer."

Grant laughed. So did Hayley. They laughed gently, in keeping with the stillness of the evening.

"What makes the splashing sounds?" Hayley asked.

"Fish jumping. Turtles dropping into the water from the shore."

"It's a living thing," Hayley said, looking at the lake. "It's full of life."

"It's . . . *alive!*" Grant said, playfully ominous.

"It's holding the moon hostage," Hayley countered, staring at the reflection of the three-quarter moon on the water.

They were quiet awhile, lost in their individual thoughts, absorbing the night.

"What did you sell?" Hayley asked, at length.

"Sell?"

"Mrs. Garth said you were a salesman."

"Computer systems." His voice was flat and bitter.

"What happened?" Hayley asked softly.

His laughter, like his earlier words, was bitter. How was he supposed to answer?

What had happened? Burnout. The breakup of a relationship that had lost its meaning and become a habit. A short war in a sand-strewn hellhole. The heroic homecoming, only to discover his accounts had been reassigned. Success to square one in just a few short steps.

"Life," he said.

Life. The one word told Hayley it was a closed subject. She studied his profile as he stared at the water. He was scarcely three feet away from her, yet he was so absorbed in thought that she wasn't sure he was even aware of her presence.

She was suddenly struck by how emotionally isolated he seemed; how alone, how troubled. No human being should be so alone. Without thinking, she put her hand on his forearm and squeezed it gently. His skin was warm, his muscles rock hard with tension.

It was not a sexual gesture. Grant understood that instantly. It was a gesture of reassurance, of one person caring for another.

Grant wished it were sexual. Sex would have been so much simpler. If the gesture had been sexual, he'd have lifted her hand to his mouth and kissed it, first the back, and then the palm. It would be very nice to kiss that cool, gentle hand; nice to kiss her lips; a bit of heaven to stretch out on the pier, bundle her next to him and bury himself in her softness, find a brief oblivion in the pleasure of it.

But the cool hand caressing his arm was not inviting sexual intimacy. It was offering emotional intimacy, and the prospect terrified Grant. Those caressing fingertips said, "I'm here. I'll listen. Talk to me."

Grant covered her hand with his to acknowledge her gesture, and sighed. It was the best he could do, all he could offer. If he started talking, he'd tell her everything, and he wasn't ready to bare his soul to anybody—especially to Hayley Addison. Hayley Addison saw too much as it was.

"Did you see your gardenia?" he asked.

"They bloomed?" Between her determination to avoid Grant all week and the confusion over Bluster's disappearance that afternoon, she hadn't had much opportunity to monitor the gardenia bed.

"One did. I found it when I was rescuing your mutt."

"I want to see," she said, getting up. "If you'll watch Bluster, I'll get a flashlight."

"Don't go all the way to your house. There's one in the truck."

He straightened his legs, and Bluster jumped up, still half asleep, and comically disoriented. Finally he barked, sounding outraged. Hayley and Grant laughed.

"You named him right," Grant said. "He's full of bluster."

The puppy followed at their heels as they strolled to the copse of gardenias. Grant aimed the beam of light toward the shrubs until he found the one blossom he'd seen earlier. Hayley gasped, and bent to examine the flower. "It's beautiful. I was expecting a lot more petals, like a rose, but it's more like an orchid."

With her nose near the bloom, she inhaled deeply. "My first gardenia," she said. "I should do something to celebrate."

"Champagne?" he suggested drolly.

"I don't even have a bottle of cheap wine."

"I have an idea. Here." He handed her the flashlight, then reached out to pluck the flower. The limb bent easily, but the bloom held fast.

Finally, it yielded. "Now what?" Hayley asked. "Do we put a candle in it, and cast it adrift in the lake, like in a Viking funeral?"

"You *are* a romantic," he said. "I don't happen to have a small candle handy, do you?" Hayley shook her head, and he said, reassuringly, "I have a better idea anyway."

He slid the flower into her hair above her right ear, then tilted her chin up, and studied her face. It was perfect.

I'm going to regret this, he thought. Nevertheless, he slid his fingertips up to caress her cheek and lowered his mouth to hers.

The sweetness of the kiss overwhelmed Hayley. She had expected urgency, not this chaste brush of his lips over hers, this gentle pressure of his fingertips on her cheek. Raising her hand to his chest, she stepped closer, impatient to feel his arms around her, as memories of her dream mingled with the reality of his mouth tenderly melting into hers.

But instead of embracing her, he ended the kiss. His fingers remained on her cheek for a few seconds, then he dropped his hand to encircle her wrist and guide her hand from his chest.

She met his gaze, questioning, and found a reflection of the regret she was feeling. They stood looking at each other until a baying puppy bark broke the mood of enchantment.

"What'd you find, Bluster?" Hayley asked. The dog barked again, then jumped clumsily backward with a yelp of distress. Hayley dashed toward him with a gasp of concern.

Grant grabbed her arm and held her back. "It could be a snake." He took the flashlight from her hands and directed the beam toward the ground near the dog, then announced, "Just a toad."

"Can it . . . hurt him?"

"Not unless it scares him to death. But if he ate it, it could make him sick."

Hayley scooped Bluster into her arms. "Behold, the big game hunter."

"I'll walk you to your door before he gets into any more trouble."

Walked to her door in the moonlight. A chaste kiss. Unfulfilled desire. It was archaic, and wildly romantic. Hayley savored the comfortable intimacy between them as they walked side by side.

It seemed fitting that he should kiss her again—no more than a brief brush of his lips—when he said good night. And that their good nights should be mere whispers. Hayley entered her house feeling replete with the romance of the entire evening. She leaned against the door and inhaled deeply, breathing in the rich fragrance of the gardenia.

Smiling, she raised her hand, tempted to touch the flower, then remembered what Slim had said about the petals bruising easily. She would have to hold it by the stem and take it out carefully.

She put Bluster down, then walked over to the decorative mirror on the living-room wall. What she saw surprised her. The damp night air had kinked her hair, and the resultant curls, along with the brilliant white flower, made her appear both innocent and exotic. Her cheeks were flushed, her eyes bright.

She looked...desirable. She smiled. *Because she had been desired.* Grant Mackenzie had drawn away, but it hadn't been because of lack of interest in her as a woman. He'd wanted to hold her as badly as she'd wanted to be held. Of that she was certain.

What it was, she told herself firmly, *was common sense. And it's a good thing one of us had the good sense to stop. Just because you dream about a man—*

She touched her lips wistfully and closed her eyes, remembering the intense sweetness of the kiss.

"Tramp!"

She spun around. Arthur Ramsey stood a few feet away from her, as sour and sanctimonious as he had been in her dream.

"You let him cheapen you!" he roared.

It's impossible! she thought. *I dreamed him, but I'm not sleeping now, I'm awake.*

"You're not here!" she cried. "You can't be."

"He'll make a tramp of you!"

Bluster, at her feet, let out a mournful yowl.

Hayley's heart was thundering, her mind anesthetized by shock and disbelief. This couldn't be happening. Bluster's howl was ear-piercing. She pressed her hands over her ears to block it out.

Arthur Ramsey did not move, but stood glaring at her with a demented expression. It was purely her instinct for survival that made Hayley reach for the nearest portable object to defend herself. Her fingers closed around a brass swan on the table beneath the mirror, and she threw it with all her might.

Despite her shattered nerves, her aim was excellent. The swan hit Arthur Ramsey's broad chest dead center—and passed without resistance straight through the area where a human heart would have been.

His expression changed, not to one of pain, but of outrage at the assault. His face red with fury, he scowled at her and uttered an angry, feral growl.

4

HAYLEY, WEAK WITH fear, could only stare back at Arthur Ramsey in frozen fascination—and watch, not daring to breathe, as he gradually vanished, until only a hint of a human form hung suspended in the air like dust particles in sunlight.

Even after the last, pale shadow had dissipated, she stood still, her entire being focused on that faded figure, feeling nothing except the shock of having witnessed the impossible, hearing nothing except the echo of his derogatory tirade, seeing nothing except the blank space where Arthur Ramsey had stood.

Eventually, Bluster's hysterical barking broke the trancelike spell. Weak-kneed, Hayley sank to the floor and drew the dog close. He was easily reassured, and in the sudden quiet it seemed to Hayley as though her senses were unnaturally keen. She could hear the muted whir of the refrigerator on the other side of the wall, the tinkle of the wind chimes on the patio, the puppy's breathing. A peculiar dank odor blended with the scent of gardenia and the pungent smell of floor wax. Hayley's eyes and chest felt as though they'd been scalded, and her throat ached with an unreleased scream.

She nestled Bluster against her midriff, conscious of his warmth and weight in her arms. Earthly warmth and earthly weight—flesh, blood, bones, muscle, all bundled together into a little scrap of a dog. In her distress, that warm bundle was Hayley's only tangible link to any other normal, mortal life. She clutched the puppy tightly and pressed her cheek against the top of his head and shivered uncontrollably.

What she had just seen was impossible. Men did not come back from the grave to insult perfect strangers. Brass swans did not pass through solid bodies. And real people did not disappear in front of your eyes. And yet—

Hayley groaned. What was the alternative? That she was lonely and impressionable and had conjured up the ghost? No. It couldn't be! True, she'd been fascinated by the story of the Ramsey girl's elopement, and the fact that Arthur Ramsey had become a hermit. It was also true that she missed her family—who wouldn't? She was living away from her parents and siblings for the first time. But she wasn't lonely to the point of becoming mentally unhinged. And she certainly didn't need to manufacture a ghost to spice up a dull existence; between a new job and a new house, her life was positively hectic.

Bluster strained against her restricting embrace and, as Hayley loosened her grip, wriggled out of her lap. Feeling as though her limbs were leaden weights, Hayley rose to her knees, and then stood.

What now? she thought, feeling detached from reality as she had always known it. Her house was haunted.

She'd seen a ghost. *Oh, God. What was she supposed to do now?*

From the kitchen came the sound of Bluster's metal food dish scraping across the floor—empty again. Sometimes she suspected the little hound was part piglet. She was thankful that the empty dish gave her something specific to do. She filled it, then leaned against the counter and watched Bluster assault the fresh food as though he hadn't eaten in a week.

"Glad to see our encounter with Arthur Ramsey hasn't affected your appetite," she grumbled, but the dog was a poor audience for sarcasm. She turned and looked out the window above the sink, through the screen walls of the Florida room toward the bait shop and the pier. Both appeared deserted, although Grant's truck was parked in its usual spot, and Hayley reasoned with a deep stab of disappointment that Grant had already burrowed into his room at the rear of the shop for the night. She hadn't realized how much she'd been hoping to see him, how desperately she'd needed the reassuring sight of a fellow human being.

She wasn't sure what she would have done if he'd been outside, sitting on the pier. Joined him, and tried to make small talk about the moonlight on the water?

Thrown herself in his arms and clung to him as though the world was coming to an end, is more like it, she thought. Her shoulders drooped as she leaned tiredly against the counter. A man's arms would feel like heaven right now, especially the arms of a man as strong as Grant Mackenzie.

She turned on the faucet, cupped her hands under the water, and splashed cold water on her face. It was probably just as well Grant was safely out of sight. She could imagine his reaction if she hurled herself against him and blurted out some hysterical story about Arthur Ramsey's ghost calling her a tramp.

Impulsively she reached for the phone and dialed her parents' number. When her mother answered, the voice and the inflection of the hello were so poignantly familiar that her mother might have been mere blocks away instead of at the other end of the country. Hayley had to choke back a lump in her throat before replying, "Mom? It's Hayley."

"Hayley? Your voice sounds funny."

"I, uh, had a frog in my throat." She cleared her throat for emphasis.

"You're not catching cold, are you?"

Her mother's concern, so typical, brought the sting of tears to Hayley's eyes—and, incredibly, a smile to her lips. "It's warm here, Mom. Nobody has a cold."

An expectant silence followed. Knowing her mother was waiting for her to explain why she'd called, Hayley searched for a feasible reason, other than that she had needed to hear a familiar voice. The metallic skid of Bluster's dish on the floor provided inspiration. "Guess what?" she said. "I got a puppy!"

After she had thoroughly described Bluster and his personality quirks, the conversation moved to the minutiae of family gossip. Hayley was brought up to date on her grandfather's bunions, her niece's latest temper tantrum, her brother-in-law's anticipated promotion at work, her infant nephew's first tooth and her sister's disastrous new haircut.

Hayley listened with growing calm. The mundane details of her loved ones' lives were comforting, like a favorite old lap blanket on a cold, dreary night. The idea of a ghost haunting her house suddenly seemed remote and ridiculous.

"Don't forget," her mother reminded her in a post-script to goodbye. "Honey, lemon juice and whiskey if that throat gets any worse."

"I won't forget, Mom," Hayley said with long-suffering tolerance. But the motherly nagging had scraped a raw nerve and she felt the lump of emotion back in her throat as she replaced the telephone receiver, severing the connection—and her link to the world as she had known it prior to the supernatural appearance of Arthur Ramsey.

AFTER A FULL DAY IN the laundry room, Bluster was so wound up and boisterous that Hayley had no choice but to take him outside to run off some of his excess energy. In the yard, he alternated between affectionate lunges at her ankles, demanding attention, and impatient forays through the grass to sniff the twisting trails of long-gone rabbits and armadilloes.

Hayley watched, amused by the intensity of his concentration as he sniffed at a tuft of clover, stopped abruptly, then energetically began to claw at the earth with his front paws. "Bluster! Stop that immediately!"

Unaccustomed to her sharp tone, the pup sat down and gave her a puzzled look. Hayley chuckled. "Sorry, boy. No digging."

Her apologetic tone was all the encouragement the pup needed to leap up and beg for attention. His paws, coated with fresh soil, pressed firmly into the pant legs of her slacks. Hayley sighed in exasperation. "It's a good thing these pants are washable or you'd be in big trouble, you little monkey."

She paid little heed to the sound of a distant door slamming, but Bluster acted as though it were the starting gun in a footrace. Before Hayley had time to react, he was off, dashing at full speed toward the bait shop. Resignedly, Hayley followed his lead at a comfortable trot, muttering about buying a collar and leash—tomorrow, on the way home from work.

She was not at all surprised to find Grant sitting on the pier, nor to discover that Bluster had found him and was cozily settled in his lap, while Grant obligingly scratched him behind the ears. She chuckled softly when the dog gave her a gloating look that seemed to say, "See, I know just how to get what I want."

At the sound of her gentle laughter, Grant turned to gaze at Hayley. Her dark tailored slacks and cream-colored blouse were crisply professional. She looked respectable, conservative, credible; like a person who could balance a set of books.

Beyond the "uniform," she looked the way a woman should look. The setting sun bathed her in a golden glow, softened her features and made a halo around her hair. Despite the mannish cut of her slacks, her silhouette was feminine—her breasts full beneath the drape of her blouse, her hips flaring gently below her belted waist. Her outfit reminded him that she was the embodiment of everything he had vowed to put behind him—but all he could think of when he stared at her was how good she'd look with no clothes on at all.

Already self-conscious over having invaded his privacy uninvited, Hayley forced herself not to fidget under Grant's speculative gaze. It wasn't easy. His stare bordered on rudeness, and there was a sensual gleam in his eyes that sent unbidden memories of her erotic dream rushing through her mind. Hoping that the waning sunlight was dim enough to mask the flush warming her face, she forced a smile and said lightly, "We've got to stop meeting like this."

He hesitated before replying, and patted the wooden planking of the pier next to his hip. "You're welcome to sit down and watch the sunset if you're not afraid of getting your pants dirty."

Hayley blanched at the inhospitable invitation. What had she done to merit his disdain? Her first impulse was to grab Bluster and flee Grant's animosity, but curiosity and a stubborn streak compelled her to stay. "They're already dirty, thanks to that little mutt you're coddling."

"Who? This little guy? He's a perfect gentleman," Grant said. "He'd never get a lady dirty."

Perfect gentleman? Dirty, rotten-hearted little traitor is more like it, Hayley thought sourly as she watched Bluster tilt his head so Grant could scratch his neck. "You didn't get him until he'd run off some of the energy he'd built up in the laundry room," she said irritably.

Grant grinned benignly. "Wild, huh?"

Hayley had settled onto the pier and was sitting Indian-style. She pinched her right stocking between thumb and forefinger and lifted it away from her ankle so that light traveled through several runs. "Destroyed, and if you think these are bad, you should see the laundry room," she replied. "His water bowl was turned over. His food was scattered from wall to wall. And you wouldn't believe what he did to the newspaper in my recycling bin. The place looks like a war zone."

"A war zone isn't shredded newspaper and spilled dog food, Hayley."

"It was only a figure of speech," Hayley said defensively, and turned to face Grant. He was staring at the water with fierce concentration, so all she saw was a profile that, except for an occasional twitch of jaw muscle, was as immobile as cast metal. He was so tense that the rise and fall of his chest as he breathed seemed exaggerated. Hayley doubted that he was conscious of the fact that he was stroking the dog's neck, and wasn't sure he'd even heard her last comment.

When he spoke, it was unexpected, and the words were so heavy with emotion that they were almost painful to hear. "War is blood, and hunger, and filth, and flies, and people so far away from everything they've ever known that nothing seems real."

"You've seen it firsthand," she said softly. It was much stronger than a guess; his emotional scars were as visible as a bleeding wound.

After a prolonged pause, he turned to face her. "I was one of those civic-minded reservists who heeded the call of duty for Desert Storm."

Hayley looked away to avoid the intensity in his eyes and studied the reflection of the sun shimmering on the rippling surface of the water.

"Another five minutes," Grant said, after a long silence.

Hayley nodded. "I still can't believe it sometimes—that I'm here, and that all this is right out the back door. It's so different from New York."

"There was a time when I took it for granted."

What was it about sharing a sunset that created instant intimacy? Hayley wasn't sure yet that she even liked Grant, but under the spell of the sinking sun, she felt as though she'd known him forever; was tuned in to his every mood and emotion; could talk to him about anything, no matter how personal. She sensed the tension in his body and shared the anguish of his troubled heart. "You don't take it for granted anymore."

It was both statement and question. Grant sighed. "I don't take anything for granted anymore."

"Was the experience so awful for you?"

"Saudi Arabia was bad. Coming home was worse."

"I don't understand," Hayley said, in a way that made it obvious she wanted to.

Grant shrugged. Why should she understand, when he sure as hell didn't? His whole life had taken a detour into a nightmare zone.

"Did something happen while you were away?"

Grant chortled bitterly. "Yeah. Something happened, all right." *Life had gone on without him as though he'd never occupied a space in it.*

The wooden planks of the pier were hard and uncomfortable. Hayley shifted, stretching her right leg out in front of her, and drawing her left leg up and hugging it. She turned her head in Grant's direction, rested her cheek on her knee and studied his face. Even at a ninety-degree angle, it was an interesting face, an intriguing combination of fine bone structure and rugged angles. His thick golden hair was touched a bit too heavily with gray at the temples for a man his age. Intriguing scars marked his forehead just above his right eyebrow and the side of his chin, but they were scars of boyhood, too old and faded to be attributable to the Gulf War.

"Were you wounded?" she asked.

"I stubbed my toe on a cot once. It hurt like hell, but the President didn't hand out a Purple Heart for it." He glanced at his watch. "Three minutes down, two to go."

His prediction was accurate. The sun had lowered until it was a ruddy ball perched on the horizon, ready to topple out of sight. Hayley watched silently as it finished its descent and gradually slid from view. The moon was already up and produced shadows and silhouettes with its silvery glow. She became aware of the night sounds again—the chirping and croaking and plopping that were losing their menace through familiarity. Even more, she was aware of Grant sitting next to her, of the warmth radiating from his body and, when she listened for it, the rhythm of his breathing. She remembered her dream, the fantasy touch of his hands on her body, and wished with a desire that was irrational yet undeniable that she could turn to him and know he would embrace her.

It should have startled her when Grant's hand settled on her shoulder, but she wasn't at all surprised. She accepted the comfort his strong fingers offered and tilted her head until her hair brushed the back of his hand. *It's the sunset,* she thought. *He's fallen under the spell of it, too.*

"Can you talk about the war?" she asked.

He waited so long to answer that she wondered if he was going to reply at all. Then he said, "You've got to understand how it was before I left. My life wasn't perfect, but it was good, and I was complacent. I guess I thought everything would go on just the way it was going, that nothing ever had to change."

He drew in a deep breath, and exhaled it slowly. "When my unit was called up, I was in shock, but I thought...*assumed*...that I could go do what needed doing, and that when I came back everything would fall back into place. I thought—"

There was another long and painful hesitation. "When we were over there, everything was . . . It was like it couldn't be happening, because it was just too awful to be real. Gas masks. Sleeping in tents. Sand. Heat. Cold. Snakes. Flies. We were all miserable, and scared, and homesick."

He toyed absently with a curl that had been teasing the top of his hand. "Thinking about going home got us through it. Especially after the firing started, and we were sleeping in MOPP suits and taking little white pills in case we got hit by nerve gas. We couldn't get away from it, ever. We just wanted to get it over with and get home."

He fell into a pensive silence. Hayley turned toward him slightly, and, covering his hand with her own, guided it from her shoulder to rest on the wooden planking between them before threading her fingers through his. "What happened when you came home?"

"You mean after the parades?"

She nodded, feeling the pain that underscored his sarcasm. Her gaze drifted to the water, where reflected moonlight bobbed on the surface like a finger of captured lightning.

Grant sounded more normal when he resumed talking. "For a while I showered three times a day and ate hamburgers and french fries for lunch and dinner. I got in my car and drove around with all the windows rolled down, just smelling the fresh air. And I went back to sleeping in a real bed, in a room with walls."

Sleeping *alone*. Late at night had been the only time he'd really missed Melissa, probably because sleeping together was the only part of their relationship that hadn't eroded from lack of nurturing before he left. Even then, he wasn't certain it was Melissa he was missing; snuggled between clean sheets in the luxury of a thermostatically-controlled climate, he'd simply yearned for some fundamental communion with a fellow human being with body parts that complemented his own. He still did—but lately, his yearnings seemed to be focused on a *particular* human being.

A gentle squeeze of his hand drew him out of the maze of thoughts into which he'd wandered. They'd been talking about something. The war, he remembered reluctantly; the war, and the revelations of his homecoming.

"Then what?" she prompted.

"I was dying to get back to work," he resumed. "I'd missed it. The people. The challenge. The competition. I was chomping at the bit to get in touch with my old accounts and reestablish my territory. That first day. . . they had the corporate headquarters decorated with yellow ribbons, and a cake with a yellow icing bow."

"They must have thought a lot of you," Hayley said.

"Oh, yes," he replied, mocking and sarcastic. "They thought a lot of me. I found out just how much they thought of me."

He paused before continuing. "For six years, I worked fourteen-hour days for that company. I started out with a phone directory and a telephone and built up the largest customer base and highest sales figures in the entire company. And then I went off to play hero."

He faced her squarely. "Tell me, Hayley, when all the reservists were out defending democracy, were you a patriotic citizen? Did you wear a yellow ribbon pinned to your lapel?"

His tone was so accusatory, Hayley found herself answering defensively. "It was my last semester of college. All the students—"

"I'll bet you believed all those yellow ribbons really meant something." He laughed bitterly. "So did we. We read about them in magazine articles. People mentioned them in letters. They were all part of the big myth."

"I'm not sure I know what you mean."

"The myth. The myth we all swallowed, hook, line and sinker. We all believed that we had a job to do, and that we were going to do it and go home. We thought we were . . . noble. God, what fools we were."

"Oh, Grant." Her chest ached with the hurt he was trying to conceal. She wasn't thinking about inviting intimacy as she raised her hands to cradle his face in them; she wasn't thinking at all, but feeling a woman's compassion for a man's vulnerability.

Grant bristled at her touch. He didn't want pity—not hers or anyone else's. But her hands were soft against his skin, and her touch was soothing, and the part of him that had been hurting for so long yearned to be comforted. He searched the depths of her eyes for deception or ridicule, and found only concern. It was mesmerizing. And to a man too long denied, irresistibly seductive.

He plunged his fingers into her hair and cradled her
head in his hands. Everything blended together as he
moved his face toward hers—the sound of the water
and the crickets; the sound of her breathing; the moist,
gardenia-scented night air, mingling with Hayley's
perfume, fresh and feminine; the moonlight captured
by the lake's surface and spilling over the lawn.

He reminded himself that she was not offering passion, but he was suddenly ravenous for anything she
could give. He was tired of denial, tired of turning away
from the very thing his soul hungered for. And Hayley
was there, touching his cheeks with her fingertips, while
moonlight danced in her eyes. Her hair felt like strands
of silk as he curled his fingers into it, and abruptly, almost violently, he pulled her face to his and pressed his
mouth to hers.

He had meant only to take comfort, but her lips
parted invitingly under his, and as he plundered the
depths of her mouth, desire swept through him, hot,
swift, compelling.

Hayley was caught off guard by the sensual on-
slaught of the kiss. He'd been so bitter, so wounded,
that her heart had gone out to him. She'd wanted to be
his friend, to let him know that she was there, willing
to listen, ready to understand. But when he'd run his
fingers through her hair, the intimacy of it had jarred
her from head to toe. Whatever her intentions had been
in reaching out to him, it was evident from her response to his touch that there was more than simple
friendship between them.

She was held captive to the kiss by a force stronger than the physical grip he had on her hair; by a force that originated deep inside her and had been awakened by his touch. It was too intense, but she couldn't bring herself to deny the passion between them; it throbbed in her veins, hot and demanding. She tried to think, but was defeated by the desire he aroused in her. She wanted to draw away, but urged him closer instead.

Each subtle surrender set Grant's heart racing with need. He urged her backward, anticipating the bliss of stretching out on the pier and cradling her entire length against him.

As anxious as he for more intimate contact, Hayley let him guide her, sliding her hands over his shoulders to caress the hard muscles of his back. Her breasts nestled against his chest and she moaned as she turned into his embrace.

An ungodly howl suddenly rent the air—a blood-curdling mournful howl. Startled, Grant jerked his head up and muttering an obscenity, searched for the source of the wild racket.

Wrested from the hypnotic effects of the kiss, Hayley lay still at first, then pulled away from Grant and sat up. She gasped as the unexpected weight of Bluster's front paws landed on her thigh.

"Damn mutt sounded like a banshee," Grant said, breathing hard from the rush of adrenaline triggered by the dog's howl.

Bluster looked at Hayley beseechingly, as though utterly confused. Under other circumstances, the puppy's perplexed expression might have been comical, but Hayley was still tingling from the kiss, and she was aware that Grant's expression had changed from shock to hostility. Hayley gave the pup a reassuring pat on the head and told Grant, "I think he was trying to protect me."

"The hound from hell," Grant muttered. "I must have startled him awake when I moved."

Suddenly self-conscious, Hayley felt her face coloring. "When I moaned, he must have been confused. I think he thought you were hurting me."

Grant's expression was grim, his features so rigid that his face might have been carved from stone.

I might have made love with this man, Hayley thought, with an overwhelming sensation of narrow escape. What did she know about him, really, except that he was a very troubled man? A *dangerously virile* troubled man. Even as she looked at his immobile features, thinking that he was a stranger to her, she was tinglingly aware of his masculine presence.

"Maybe he did rescue you," Grant replied, looking her straight in the eye. "You know what would have happened if he hadn't interrupted us."

Hayley nodded, and looked away, wondering if he was at least a bit disappointed. Was he hoping, even a little, that she would give him some indication that she'd be willing to pick up where they'd left off? Was this bitter, disillusioned man with the stoic expression capable of formulating a wish? Or would wishing be too painful?

She couldn't sit there any longer, embarrassed, wondering about him, tempted by him. She rose, and looked at the surface of the lake, dark now except for the shimmering reflections of moonlight and stars. "Thanks for the sunset."

Grant, leaning back on his elbows, was staring at the sky. "No charge."

Hayley picked up Bluster and cradled the dog in her arms. She didn't look at Grant. "If you happen to see Slim, please tell him I'm anxious to talk to him about the dog run. I want to get Bluster out of the laundry room as soon as possible."

"I'll flag him down if I see him."

"Thanks." She moved down the dock, anxious to be away.

"Hayley?"

She stopped and turned.

"You can leave the mutt with me during the day. Until you get the dog run up."

The offer was tempting. Hayley didn't like confining Bluster in a small room all day. But she didn't want to be indebted to Grant, and she didn't want to become involved in a situation that would necessitate her seeing him twice a day. "I couldn't ask you to do that. It would be too much—"

Grant stood. "I wouldn't mind." He was quietly intense, almost pleading.

He's lonely, she suddenly realized. It seemed incredible—and yet, it made perfect sense. He'd made the grandiose gesture of cutting himself off from society, and now he was just plain lonely. Lonely, and too proud to do anything about it, except volunteer to puppy-sit.

"I like to get to the office early."

"Naturally," was the disdainful reply.

Back to your usual charming self, eh, Mackenzie? Hayley thought, but did not acknowledge the barb. "I leave home before seven."

"Just bring him over. I'll be up."

"Well, Bluster, looks like you've got a date tomorrow morning," Hayley told the dog as she set him down in her living room. "No more laundry room. Speaking of which—" She sighed, thinking of the mess she had to clean up. "You stay out of trouble. I'm going to change into something more comfortable and then whip us up some dinner."

She placed her hands on her hips in a challenging stance and said loudly, "And *you*, Arthur Ramsey, if you're listening, don't even consider showing up and calling me names. I am in *no* mood for any of your shenanigans tonight."

She felt quite brave standing there, defiantly ordering a ghost not to haunt her—until a horrible crashing noise in the next room startled her into an involuntary shriek. Maybe the cavalier approach was a bit rash, she reflected, as her heart lodged in her throat.

Trembling, she stole to the kitchen door to investigate, then heaved a sigh of relief, before sternly scolding, "Bluster! No! How many times do I have to tell you not to play in the trash can?"

5

"I'M SORRY ABOUT THIS," Lora said.

Hayley, seated behind her desk, shrugged. "The books have to be closed out."

"I'd stay and help, but my daughter's dance class is ordering recital costumes tonight, and if I don't take her with checkbook in hand, she won't be able to participate in the recital." She tucked her purse under her arm, then looked at Hayley and sighed. "You didn't have plans for tonight, did you?"

"Just a lonely microwave dinner in front of the television."

"Why don't I believe that?" Lora asked wryly.

"Because married people think single people have a nonstop party they tap in to the moment they leave the office."

Lora laughed. "With the hours you put in here, you couldn't possibly have energy left over for any heavy-duty partying. Well—see you in the morning."

An eerie silence descended over the office after Lora had gone. There were other employees in the building, but they were several doors away. Hayley propped her elbows on her desk and her chin on her fists. Her eyes were tired from the glare of the computer monitor, her behind was sore from sitting, her shoulders were knotted with tension, and her stomach was rumbling reminders that it had been five hours since lunch. And she had a solid two hours' work to do before she could go home.

She turned on the small radio she kept on her desk to keep from feeling so isolated, and scrolled a new file onto the computer monitor. A dozen or so files later, she stopped to stretch. On the radio the traffic reporter was signing off, reminding Hayley that most of the nine-to-five crowd were already home—and she had another hour's work to do. At least Bluster wasn't locked up inside that tiny laundry room.

Bluster! Where was her brain? She hadn't even thought about calling Grant to let him know she'd be late. What if he had plans?

Luckily, his number was listed with Information. He picked the phone on the sixth ring and barked an inhospitable hello.

Hayley returned a tentative, "Hi, Grant. It's Hayley."

"Oh, Hayley. Hi."

Was it her imagination, or did he actually sound glad to hear from her? "I have to stay late to finish up some accounts, and it occurred to me that we don't have a contingency plan for Bluster in case you need to go somewhere when I'm not home at the usual time."

"As a matter of fact, I have a hot dinner date. I thought I'd just drown the mutt if you weren't back by the time I'm ready to leave."

"Drown?" Hayley echoed weakly as the blood drained from her face.

"It was a *joke*, Hayley," Grant said, his irritation apparent even through the phone line. "I'm not in the habit of drowning helpless puppies."

"I didn't really think—"

"Yes, you did!"

"You surprised me," she said. "I wasn't expecting a joke."

There was a brooding silence at the other end of the line. Hayley tried again. "Would I have left Bluster with you if I'd thought there was any danger of your hurting him?"

After an awkward hesitation, he said, "So you're working late."

"It's the closing date for one of our cycles."

"It's not worth it, Hayley."

Hayley bristled at his meddlesome attitude. "Is it a problem? With Bluster, I mean?"

"No. He and I were outside watching the sun go down."

"Oh." It was almost a sigh. Hayley looked at the waning sunlight filtering through the slats of the miniblinds and envied them their vantage point.

As though he'd read her mind, Grant goaded, "Do they pay you overtime for working late?"

"They pay me to do a job. I like to do it."

"If you think anyone in that big insurance company's going to notice all that dedication and hard work, you're in for a rude awakening."

"They'd notice if I didn't do my job."

"Quick enough to bounce your cute little butt right out the door faster than you can say 'unemployment,'" he assured her.

"Which is exactly why I'd better get back to work. I'll be home as soon as possible."

"Hayley?" He spoke her name after they'd exchanged goodbyes and Hayley was removing the phone from her ear.

"Hmm?"

"Don't expect them to appreciate it. You won't get anything but heartache if you expect a big corporation to give a damn about you."

There was an abrupt click and Hayley was left puzzling over their strange conversation. She'd been on the verge of telling him to mind his own business—and would have, if it wasn't for the fact that he was doing her a favor by puppy-sitting Bluster. Yet his last warning had sounded sincere; in his own boorish way he'd been trying to offer her some helpful advice. His manner might be brash, but her intuition told her that his intentions were good.

As she replaced the receiver, Hayley vowed to find out what had soured Grant Mackenzie so thoroughly on life.

HAYLEY HALF EXPECTED to find Grant and Bluster sitting on the pier when she arrived home a couple of hours later, but they were on the porch of the bait shop instead. Bluster, wagging his tail enthusiastically, dashed out to meet her as she approached. Grant, settled comfortably in one of two old-fashioned wooden rocking chairs on the porch, did not get up, but motioned to the second rocker. "It's a nice night. Come on up and sit for a spell."

Juggling to keep a flat, square box out of Bluster's reach as she knelt to pet him, Hayley looked at Grant. "Only if you promise to help me eat this pizza."

"Honey, right now I'm hungry enough to help you eat an alligator if one crawled up on the pier."

Grinning, she rose and walked toward the porch, with the puppy at her heels. "Then I'm glad I stopped at the pizzeria. Hope you like pepperoni and mushrooms."

She settled into the empty chair, opened the box and offered him the first slice. "Where'd you get the rockers?" she asked.

Grant, who was devouring pizza at an astonishing rate, paused between bites to answer, "They were in the storage shed. Finally worked my way into the far corner and found them stacked piggyback and covered with a tarp. Slim had said they must be around somewhere. Apparently they were a popular item with the customers when O'Keefe was running the shop."

Hayley leaned her head against the high back of the chair and closed her eyes. "There's something soothing about sitting in a rocking chair," she said. She hadn't realized how wound up she was until she felt the tension gradually ebbing from her muscles.

"Mmm-hmm," Grant agreed, no longer concentrating on the pizza that had tasted so good. Food had appeased one appetite, but Hayley Addison was awakening another. He was struck by her vulnerability as she sat with her eyes closed and her head tilted back. The pale column of her exposed neck made him hunger for the taste of her skin against his lips. He remembered well the texture of her skin, what she smelled like, the way she'd responded to his touch.

He'd been a fool to give her that first moonlit kiss. He was helpless now to reverse the process the kiss had set off. She haunted his thoughts and his dreams. Desire for her was embedded in his system, hot and volatile as an active volcano. And every time he told himself how wrong it was to want her, he wanted her a little more.

She opened her eyes, caught him staring and smiled self-consciously. "What's burning in the bucket?" she asked, referring to a small tin bucket that appeared to be filled with wax.

"Citronella candle. It's supposed to repel mosquitoes."

"Does it work?" She reached for a fresh piece of pizza.

"It mildly discourages them," he said wryly, also reaching for another slice of pizza.

Neither spoke again until they quibbled over who would get the last piece of the pizza. Grant thought Hayley should eat it since he'd already had half, but Hayley insisted he take it.

She watched him eat it. She was very aware of his masculinity: his size, his strength, the way he moved with an economy of motion and single-minded determination. He had nice hands, large and graceful, with well-shaped fingers. Hayley knew how gentle those hands could be. She knew how they could make her feel. Her face warmed with the memory of it.

The silence into which they'd fallen was comfortable in spite of the fact that it was filled with awareness of the attraction between them. They seemed to have an unspoken agreement that they would neither deny it nor discuss it.

Finally Hayley said, "You were pretty judgmental about my working late."

Grant frowned sullenly. "Sorry."

"You're trying to protect me," she said gently.

Grant tensed, as if he'd been accused of a crime. "I hate seeing anyone on a road to self-destruction."

"Wanting to do my job is self-destructive?"

His eyes reflected a deep hurt. "It is if you expect anyone to notice or give a damn."

Hayley opened her mouth to protest, but Grant was wound up. His words rushed out, as though they'd been dammed up inside him and could no longer be contained. "I see you all wide-eyed and filled with ambition and I see myself, just a few years ago. I'm trying to warn you, Hayley. To save you from—"

"From what happened to you?" Leaning forward, she took Grant's hand in hers and curled her fingers around his. "What did they do to you, Grant? Fire you?"

Grant laughed. "Fire me? Firing me would have been too humane."

"What, then?"

He smiled sadly, mockingly, and raised his free hand to touch her face. "Look at you. Little Miss Stars in Her Eyes. Go to school, do your job well, you'll move up the corporate ladder. You don't realize that they play games, that they use people and then throw them away. You think firing someone is the worst thing they can do to a person. Firing would be quick and merciful compared to the tortures they put people through.

She wove her fingers through his. "I'm trying to understand."

"Don't give me any of your bleeding-heart sympathy, Hayley. I don't need it. I'm out of it now. If you want to worry about someone, then watch your own back. And when you find a knife sticking out of it, don't say I didn't try to warn you."

"You may have dropped out of it, Grant, but you're not over it."

"It's a closed chapter."

"It's not a closed chapter. It's a gaping wound."

Grant's throat convulsed and he turned his head away from her. "Just do me a favor and don't come at me with any first-aid kits, okay?"

That he couldn't face her was significant. Tears of sadness stung her eyes. She exhaled a soft sigh, and said, "I won't."

He jerked his head around to look at her, and studied her face intently. She could keenly sense his inner turmoil. Comforting him would be so much easier than ignoring that something was tearing him apart inside.

"Hayley." The name was a desperate plea.

Rising from the chair, he opened his arms to her. She rushed into his embrace and slid her own arms around his neck as he drew her close. Despite the physical strength of his hard body, she felt there was an ache in him that cried out for soothing, a desperation in his kiss that begged for solace.

Without hesitation, Hayley gave everything his kiss cried out for, wanting to share her inner strength and soothe the turmoil raging within him. She let him cling to her, and she clung to him, communicating with her physical closeness what she could never have communicated with vacuous words and phrases.

The kiss ended, and still they held each other. Hayley rested her cheek against Grant's chest. She was content there, listening to the swift, steady beat of his heart.

Grant buried his face in Hayley's hair and breathed in the clean scent of it. Holding a woman had never felt so right. She fit so well, snuggled warmly against him with her breasts pressed into his ribs and her head tucked beneath his chin.

As though she belonged there, he thought, and immediately dismissed the notion. He was lonely, plain and simple. Lonely, and disillusioned. And she was there, caring and within reach.

Too caring, and too close for her own good. He closed his eyes, and for just a few seconds more, reveled in the sweetness of having her in his arms. Then, after pressing a gentle kiss on her temple, he slid his hands down her arms and reluctantly took a step backward. She looked up at him, slightly puzzled.

"I'm not going to take advantage of you, Hayley."

"I'm not worried."

He laughed—the bitter, self-denigrating laughter that was becoming all too familiar—and jammed his hands into the back pockets of his jeans. "Maybe you should be."

Hayley slipped her arms around his waist and, tilting her head back so she could see his face, smiled. "I don't think so."

She felt his muscles tense as her body aligned with his, and felt the vibration of his chest as he drew in a ragged breath. "You're making it hard for me to remember why I shouldn't take advantage of you."

His hands were still in his pockets, as though he was afraid of what he'd do if he allowed himself to touch her again. The hot, hard evidence of his wanting pressing against her belly was threatening as well as exciting—not because she was afraid he would take her by force, but because she knew he wouldn't have to. She felt his sexual hunger as keenly as she felt his pain and turmoil; and, just as the pain made her want to comfort him, the sexual hunger triggered within her a dangerous, reckless yearning for satisfaction. The need inside her was every bit as real and persistent as the hardness pressing against her.

The choice was hers. He'd pulled away, but he was as vulnerable to her because of the attraction between them as she was to him. She dropped her forehead onto his chest and sighed. The warmth and solidity of his body invited her to cuddle closer, but she resisted. She didn't fully understand the affinity between them, the empathy that enabled her to share this complicated man's innermost pain and yearning, but she suspected that it was as rare as it was intense. The same intuition told her that rushing it would be a mistake.

Drawing away from Grant was not easy. Hayley lifted her head from his chest and withdrew her arms from around his waist with regret. To hide her confusion, she rose up on tiptoe and kissed his cheek. "It's time I went home, and I'm sure Bluster's more than worn out his welcome."

Quick as lightning, Grant pulled his right hand from his pocket and grabbed her elbow to command her attention. "It's not that I don't find you attractive."

She grinned devilishly. "I know."

Her candor left him speechless. Of course, she knew; the way she'd been snuggled against him, there was no way she could have avoided noticing his arousal.

"It's all right," she said, and sighed. "Look, Grant. We're both a little ... vulnerable right now. I'm a bit lonely away from my family, and you ... Well, you've got your own set of problems. And there's some crazy kind of chemistry between us that tends to ... *erupt* every so often, but—"

"I couldn't have said it better myself," Grant told her.

"I need a friend," Hayley said. "And I have a feeling you could use a friend, too."

A friend. Something uncoiled in Grant's chest, a familiar tightness he hadn't labeled, but now had a name for: loneliness. God, how long he had been lonely? Since the war? Since before the war? He hadn't even known he was lonely. He'd had a live-in lover and legions of business associates, and he'd thought his life was full, only to discover it was as empty as Mother Hubbard's cupboard.

And now, looking into Hayley Addison's eyes, he wasn't sure he'd ever had a real friend. Too choked up to speak, he simply nodded. Friends. It was a start.

She acknowledged his nod with a gentle smile before she knelt to call her dog. She laughed aloud as the excited pup wriggled, leaped and romped with exuberance. At length, still laughing, she scooped Bluster into her arms and stroked him to calm him. With laughter lingering in her eyes, she looked at Grant over the dog's head. "Good night."

"Good night," he said, but as she started down the path toward her house, carrying the dog in her arms, he realized that he wasn't ready for her to go. He called her name, and she turned expectantly.

What prompts a man to talk of things he has never spoken of before? he wondered. He didn't consciously decide to do so. Perhaps it was simply that she had offered friendship when he'd been so long without a friend. But he was as surprised as she to hear himself saying, "They gave away my sales territory."

She seemed to understand that it was just the beginning of a long story. Without speaking, she walked back to the porch and dropped into one of the rockers. Bluster curled up in her lap and she petted his back with long strokes.

Grant settled into the other chair, and matched the rhythmic rocking of his chair to the slow pace of hers. It struck him then how attuned they were to each other. He had never experienced this type of rapport with a woman.

Finally, he continued. "I started with the company right out of college, and spent the next five years hustling my way to the top of the sales force. Computer technology was changing practically daily. The progressive companies who'd invested in computers early on were constantly upgrading to stay current, and the conservative companies who'd waited until computers had proved their value were ripe for exploitation. It was a matter of finding the right person in the company and selling our product. And I was good at selling—good enough to be top grosser for three years running."

He paused thoughtfully, and slowly shook his head. "I made money. I was so busy making money that I didn't have time to spend it, and even if I had, I didn't have anything to spend it on. The woman I was living with made plenty of money and she seemed to think it was...I don't know...a put-down or something to accept anything from me. I bought a condo and a car and stereo, and then I hired an investment counselor to invest what was left over and make more money from it. The bottom line on my portfolio became a sort of yardstick for how successful I was. That, and the awards I won for Salesman of the Year."

He looked her squarely in the eye. "So you see, my work was everything. It was all I'd done since college. Hell, I wouldn't have been playing soldier in the first place if one of my best customers hadn't been a colonel in the reserves and urged me to sign up. I made points with him, and made a lot of other contacts at the same time. And then the Gulf business came up, and we were one of the first units called up. Remember, I told you how we all focused on home?"

"I remember," Hayley said.

"We lived to get out of that desert and get home. And home to me was work. It wasn't just a job, it was my life."

He stopped to draw in a breath. "When I found out I was leaving, the owner of the company and some of the top brass took me out to dinner. They gave me a watch—shockproof, waterproof and sandproof—and made a lot of speeches about how much they'd miss me, and how my job would be waiting for me the day I came back."

"But it wasn't."

"Oh, technically it was the same job. Salesman. Of course, they'd had to reassign my territory. I had expected that. Someone had to take care of it while I was away. I just thought—I'd spent five years making it the most lucrative territory."

"And they didn't give it back to you."

"Oh, they were charming. There was a general sales meeting, and they had a cake and welcomed me back with open arms. But when I mentioned getting my territory back, there was another quiet, private little dinner with the company brass. They understood how I felt, and they appreciated all that I had done for the company. But they'd had to shake up the territory when I'd left, and they thought it would be disruptive if they made another change.

"Disruptive! God! *My* contacts. *My* accounts. And they didn't want to *disrupt* the territory. They appealed to my sense of fairness. The man who'd replaced me was doing a good job, and it would be an insult to pull him out."

He laughed bitterly. "I found out later he was making two percentage points less commission than I'd been making. The only 'fairness' they were concerned with was the dollars-and-cents kind. They explained how tight the economy had gotten, and how they'd had to reduce their sales force. Hell, they made it sound as though they were doing me a favor taking me back. Then they went into a song and dance about how valuable I was to the company, and how they were sure I would do well anywhere they put me, and how they knew I loved a challenge. So they gave me a crap territory where several entry-level hirees had struck out, and expressed supreme confidence that I would turn it around."

He exhaled a weary sigh. "I gave it my damndest, even though it was obvious why it was a crap territory. It was in a depressed area, with companies who'd been there forever. They either already had systems, or never would. P. T. Barnum couldn't have sold tickets to his circus in that territory. I requested a reassignment, and had to wait several months. The next territory was a little better. Some, but not much. I did better than anyone else had ever done there, but I was barely earning the minimum draw. The next time I requested a reassignment, they hemmed and hawed. When I resubmitted the request a couple of months later, they pointed out that my stats had been disappointing since I'd returned from the Gulf. *Disappointing.* That's when I told them to take their job and shove it, and walked off."

"My dad used to joke about doing that," Hayley said, her affection for her father evident. "Of course, he couldn't afford to actually do it with a family to support."

"Yeah. Well, I didn't have to worry about that." He'd had no roots, no ties; nothing beyond the mortgage payment on his condo and the local power company.

Hayley was curious about the woman he'd been living with. The independent, successful woman. But she refrained from asking. Instead, she asked, "Do you have family around?"

"My parents were divorced when I was a baby. Mom remarried when I was in college and moved to Washington State with my stepfather."

"And your dad?"

"I didn't see much of him when I was growing up. That hasn't changed."

"How sad for you."

Grant shrugged away her sympathy. "You can't miss what you never had. Mom and I did all right. I wasn't neglected or abused."

Again Hayley wondered about the woman he'd lived with. Again, she didn't ask. Grant appeared to be immersed in thoughts he'd rather not be thinking. Flattered that he'd opened up as much as he had, Hayley silently digested what he'd told her. She understood how he could feel betrayed, but his bitterness ran deeper than one bad break on a job. A man with his track record could undoubtedly have found a new job with a different company. But Grant Mackenzie had dropped out of life completely.

She opened her mouth to speak, then reconsidered and drew in a deep breath instead. She listened to the quiet lap of the water against the shore and wondered how he'd react to the question she'd almost asked. He might think she was meddling. Then, remembering that he'd had no qualms about butting in on her decision to work late, she decided to go for it.

"Have you ever considered counseling?"

Grant chortled in surprise. "Counseling? You mean like a shrink?" There was no bitterness in his laughter. "I don't need any shrinks, Hayley."

"The Veterans Administration would probably refer you to someone who specializes in readjustment."

"What's wrong, Hayley? Worried that I'm going to crack some night and break into your house and murder you in your sleep?"

"No, I—"

He read the horror in her eyes, and became even more serious. "I'm not going to hurt myself, either, if that's what you're worried about."

Her silence confirmed his suspicions that she had been thinking he might be suicidal. The idea chafed his pride. "Hell, Hayley, what I did was based on a healthy instinct. You said yourself that your dad always wanted to do exactly what I did. I just had the guts and the freedom to do it."

"I was just—"

"You won't see me in any psychiatrist's office. I'll stay away and make space for the people who subject themselves to stress. Who knows? You could end up on the couch yourself in a few years. Working late. Going to school. Doing whatever it takes to get ahead."

"There's nothing abnormal about wanting to get ahead."

"You're going to get awfully tired. And you're going to be awfully disillusioned when you realize you're just a number on a payroll stub to the people you're knocking yourself out for. How do you know you can handle that when it happens?"

"I won't quit my job and open a bait shop."

Grant shrugged. "I don't imagine you will."

Hayley grinned, a quirky little grin, and said in a conspiratorial whisper, "I'll open a shop that sells nothing but stuffed animals."

"You mean like teddy bears and rabbits?"

Hayley nodded. Grant threw back his head and laughed.

As his laughter echoed over the water, Hayley would have liked nothing more than to throw her arms around Grant and kiss him as if there was no tomorrow. If Bluster hadn't been asleep in her lap, she might have. Instead, she laughed along with him.

She left a few minutes later. Ordinarily she would have changed from her work clothes into a pair of shorts and a T-shirt, but since it was almost bedtime, she took a bubble bath and then slipped into a sleep shirt, feeling frivolous and self-indulgent as the satin settled over her oil-softened skin.

She usually watched the evening news before tucking in for the night, but the warm, scented bath, the extended workday and relaxing interlude on the porch had left her enervated, so she went directly to bed and planned to catch up on some letter writing before going to sleep. "Dear Grandma Addison," was as far as she got before putting her stationery aside. How could she write a letter to her grandmother, when her mind was on Grant Mackenzie?

The sheets were still cool as she cuddled down between them, but the satin sleep shirt was warm and slick against her skin and Hayley felt unbelievably sexy— even a little wicked. She drifted to sleep thinking about being kissed by Grant Mackenzie. And where memory left off, fantasy took flight....

The next thing Hayley knew, she was sitting up in bed, terrified and struggling for breath. She couldn't remember what she had dreamed, or what horrors had invaded her sleep to leave her shaking so, but the bedding was twisted and disheveled, and her heart was pounding almost painfully. The bedside light was still on. The alarm clock showed that it was not quite four o'clock.

Bluster whined and, startled, Hayley swung around to look down at him. Before she could pick him up a loud, violent knock sounded at the front door. She jerked the sheets up to her neck and stared in terror at the door that led from her bedroom to the hallway and the front door.

There was another knock, and another. Shaken from her stupor finally, Hayley reached for the phone. But as she picked up the receiver, she heard her name being called. Grant's voice. Frantic. He knocked harder, shouted louder.

Hayley sprang from the bed, dashed to the front door, and flung it open.

"Hay—" The second syllable of her name lodged in his throat when he caught sight of her. After an interval of paralyzed shock, he stepped inside and pulled her roughly into his arms. "Thank God, you're all right."

Hayley clung to him, absorbing his strength. He kissed her hair and her temple. He was winded from the run to her house, and when he spoke between kisses, his voice had a breathless quality. "When I heard the shot—"

"What shot?" Her voice was no more than a frightened whisper.

He lifted his head in surprise. "Didn't you hear it? It woke me from a sound sleep. And then I heard you scream."

"I had a nightmare. Something woke me up, but I don't think I screamed."

He jammed his fingers through his hair. "I came awake instantly. I was so sure—"

"Sound does funny things on the water. It could have come from the other side of the lake."

He shook his head. "The water may have amplified it, but it came from this direction. Could have been a car backfiring on the highway, I suppose." He didn't sound convinced.

"Maybe it's what woke me up."

"I heard you scream."

"If I did, it was in my sleep."

"Do you do that? Talk in your sleep? *Scream* in your sleep?"

"Not that I know of. But I've never had—" She thought of her erotic dream and Arthur Ramsey's ugly name-calling. Of Arthur Ramsey standing at the foot of her bed even after she awakened. Of Arthur Ramsey in her entryway, calling her names. Nightmare, hallucination or reality? "Weird dreams before," she finished lamely, wishing she could confide in him.

He ran his hand through his hair again. "I haven't slept well since . . . the desert. I would have sworn—" He sighed, then forced a smile. "You're all right. That's what matters."

Hayley wasn't at all convinced she was all right, but she nodded.

With the crisis past, Hayley became increasingly aware of the intimacy of their situation. It was the middle of the night, and they were alone. Grant's chest was bare, his tattered denim cutoffs were scarcely more substantial than a loincloth, and the satin sleep shirt that had felt so wonderfully sensual to her earlier now seemed like a blatant invitation.

She looked up at him, and the gleam in his eye confirmed that his thoughts were racing along the same treacherous path as hers. "Grant," she said hoarsely, but it was too little, too late to stop the runaway attraction that drew them together.

6

FROM THE SECOND THEIR lips joined, the kiss was intense and almost unbearably intimate. The hair on Grant's chest chafed Hayley's breasts through the soft satin of her shirt. His bare knees pressed into her naked thighs, his back muscles were smooth and hard under her grasping fingertips.

Groaning impatiently, he coaxed her mouth open, and foraged its secrets with his tongue. Hayley gave a throaty whimper as he deepened the kiss. He cupped her bottom with one hand and pulled her so tightly against his hardness that the zipper of his pants scraped her stomach. She didn't feel pain—only the thrilling heat and rock hardness of him, the dizzying realization that she had evoked this powerful desire in him, and the answering excitement of passion pulsing inside her.

Grant couldn't seem to get close enough to her. His gut-wrenching fear for her safety and overwhelming relief at finding her safe fed the desire for her that had been festering in him since the first time he'd seen her.

Her breasts, warm and lush, pressed into his chest through her sleep shirt as she clung to him. Heavenly sensations, hellish frustration. The slippery shiny little scrap she wore was just substantial enough to frustrate his desperate yearning to feel naked skin against naked skin.

He slid his hand down from her buttocks until he encountered bare flesh beneath the hem of that ridiculous skimpy shirt. The fabric bunched above his hand as he traced her thigh up to her hip with his palm. His fingers spanned womanly curves and angles: the swell of buttocks, the taper from hip to waist, the hollow at the base of her spine. He tore his mouth from hers to sample the delicate skin of her neck. Her languid sigh, warm and moist, teased his ear.

And then it registered in his passion-fogged brain that she was pulling away from him, pushing on his chest with the heels of her hands. It was a mistake. It had to be. She couldn't be pulling away. Not after the way she had melted against him. Not after the sounds of pleasure she'd made, the way she'd ignited at his touch.

"We can't do this," she said, her voice hoarse. Her face was flushed with arousal.

"You can't be serious." His breath was coming in hard gulps.

"Not now. Not like this."

"Right now. Just like this."

"I'm not . . . prepared."

That gave him pause. His power of reasoning slowly returned.

"Are you?" she challenged.

"I was in a hurry to save your life," he said testily, then sheepishly admitted, "I don't even have my keys in my pocket."

She closed her eyes and groaned.

"Yeah," he said. "Me, too."

Hayley opened her eyes. "It wouldn't have been a good idea, even if we had been prepared."

Grant snorted skeptically.

"Tonight on the porch, you didn't want to take advantage of me," she continued. "If we made love now, we might be taking advantage of each other. We—"

"Hayley," he interrupted, and the word held a warning. "Shut up."

The dangerous glint in his eyes was enough to convince Hayley it would be folly to cross him. She nodded meekly, and the charged silence that followed seemed to go on forever.

Finally, Grant made a sound in his throat that was suspiciously like a growl, then announced bluntly, "I'm leaving."

They walked to the door together. Grant moved to open the door, then paused with his hand on the knob. "When I thought something had happened to you—"

She was looking at him with wide, sleepy eyes, and the picture she presented—flushed, disheveled and sexily clad—made him ache to possess her. Mentally cursing his conscience—the only thing stopping him from grabbing her and kissing her into mindless submission—he forced himself to open the door. But he lingered there, not quite able to leave. "I didn't plan on this. On you. On—"

She had a stricken expression on her face, as though she might burst into tears. "Are you sure you're all right?"

"Yes!" He hesitated. "No. I—"

She sighed, and the soft fabric of her shirt fluttered between her breasts. Her nipples, still pebbled, were clearly delineated under the satin, and Grant had to force his gaze to her face. "What is it?" he asked.

"I just— Would it be— Could you hug me, just for a moment? Just . . . hug me?"

"And not pounce on you like a drunken sailor on shore leave?" The words held more self-loathing than sarcasm. "I wouldn't be much of a man if I couldn't comfort a woman who needs comforting, would I?"

She answered by sliding her arms around his waist and nestling her cheek against his chest. He cradled her head in his right palm, combing his fingers into her curls, and rested his chin just above her temple. Her presence filled his senses—the scent of her hair and the lushness of her breasts against his ribs. He was surprised by the trust she placed in him by putting her arms around him.

Earlier, when he'd thought she was in danger, he would have killed to protect this woman. Now, he'd kill himself before he violated her trust. He'd needed to hug her as much as she'd needed to be hugged. Surprisingly, it felt good to acknowledge need, as though he'd regained a part of himself that he'd been out of touch with for some time.

He held her until he felt the tension leave her body. "Feel better?"

"Mmm-hmm," she said, sounding wonderfully sleepy.

"I think that's my cue to leave," he said wryly.

"'Fraid so," she murmured, burrowing her cheek against his chest.

"Uh-uh. None of that." He grasped her shoulders and very gently guided her away from him. "I'm only human, you know."

"I think you're—"

"Shh," he said, then bent forward to kiss her cheek. "If you start talking, you'll only wake yourself up." *And drive me a little more insane,* he thought. "Good night, Hayley."

"Good night."

"Lock the door."

She nodded.

"And get some sleep."

"Gladly," she said, covering a huge yawn with the back of her hand. She locked the door, returned to bed and pulled the covers around her like a cocoon. Bouncing her head around on the pillow a few times, searching for an ideal position, she reflected that if she hadn't sent Grant away, she could have been cuddling up to him instead.

You didn't have any problem getting comfortable next to him. The thought drifted into her mind during that stage of drowsiness that precedes sleep. Almost as if to mock that private thought, a whisper rose from the darkness.

"Shameless tramp!"

Hayley groaned. She couldn't see him, but the voice was unmistakable. "Oh, give it a rest, you old fart! I am *not* your daughter!"

She yanked the covers over her head, determined to ignore Arthur Ramsey. Let him find some other house to haunt. After waking up in the middle of the night from a nightmare and almost having unprotected sex with Grant Mackenzie on the living room floor, she was in no mood for any prudish ghost nonsense.

Something like a whirlwind blew through the room and whipped at the bedding, but Hayley held it firmly around her until the tempest subsided, hoping that Arthur remained true to his past pattern of irritating but harmless name-calling. The stillness that followed provided only a few seconds of reprieve before a bloodcurdling howl rent the still air.

Bluster. What else tonight? Exhausted, she called to him. Ignoring her rules, he propped his front paws against the edge of the bed and whimpered pitifully; she broke the rules, too, by lifting him onto the bed.

She welcomed his warm little presence curled up next to her as she finally drifted off to sleep.

WHEN THE SNOOZE ALARM on Hayley's clock went off for the third time the next morning, her head felt as though she'd been on a weekend booze binge. She had to drag herself out of bed and into the shower. The mad frenzy to get ready for work left little opportunity to dwell on what would happen when she had to face

Grant again after their aborted lovemaking of the night before.

Mercifully, she didn't have to get close enough to worry. When she and Bluster went out her back door, he was sitting in a rocker on the bait-shop porch, drinking coffee. Hayley let Bluster run to greet him, and called, "I'm running late."

Rising, Grant waved. "Go on. I'll corral the mutt."

With a heartfelt, "Thanks," Hayley dashed to her car. If she got a few lucky breaks in the traffic, she might make it to work on time.

It was a miserable day. Tired from too little sleep, Hayley found it difficult to concentrate on her work and all too easy to dwell on the events of the night before. Somehow, in the middle of the night, when she was groggy from sleep and shaken by Grant's unexpected arrival, the theory that Grant had mistaken a car's backfire for a shot and a wild animal cry for a scream had seemed more viable. By light of day, the entire episode took on ominous and mysterious overtones that fit all too well with the scenario of nightmares and a haunted house. She didn't know *how* it fit, she just knew that it did.

Then there was her resident ghost. Old Arthur hadn't proved dangerous so far, but his appearances were disconcerting and his nagging insults were downright irritating. Obviously he had her confused with his daughter. If she could convince him that she wasn't her, maybe he'd leave. But how was she supposed to go about convincing him? As tiresome as Arthur Ramsey and his insults were, she disliked the prospect of calling in psychics or mediums.

What had the Ramsey girl been like? Hayley wondered. A strong physical resemblance might explain why Arthur kept confusing Hayley with his daughter. Admittedly, it would be a long shot—a truth-is-stranger-than-fiction coincidence—but Hayley vowed to find out everything she could about Ramsey's daughter.

Equally as troublesome and of far more immediate concern was what had happened or, more precisely, what had *almost* happened, between her and Grant. She was physically attracted to him. That was fact. And the more time she spent with him, the more attracted she became. At the same time, she was wary of Grant Mackenzie. He was a complex, troubled man and it would be unwise to get too close, emotionally, to a man with so many problems. But while her head was busy doubting the wisdom of getting closer to him, her heart yearned to understand him, and her body ached for the physical fulfillment of his lovemaking.

Living with her parents had always given Hayley a safety net when it came to men. There had been no awkward decisions to make over whether to invite a man in at the end of an evening. If her date came in with her, it was for a soda or hot chocolate, consumed in the living room, usually with her parents in attendance. When she decided to become intimate with a man, the decision to do so had been well thought out—and she had been totally discreet out of respect for her parents.

There had been no overnight stays, no long weekends at his place.

She hadn't felt stifled by remaining so close to her parents, but she had often fantasized about what her life would be like without their constant supervision. She'd thought about it even more often during the months she was preparing for her move. She'd imagined herself giving parties, not worrying about how late she stayed out, inviting sophisticated men in for a glass of wine, and dancing to mellow music on the stereo.

But nothing in her fantasies had prepared her for having a bare-chested Grant Mackenzie beating on her door in the middle of the night and hugging her while she was in her skimpiest nightie. Nor had she ever considered the aphrodisiac effects of watching the sun set over a lake with a man who was sexy as a satyr—and bitter, lonely and vulnerable and...nice, all at the same time.

She was going to have to face Grant sooner or later. That thought was uppermost in her mind as she started the drive home after work. Would they discuss what had happened? Would they ignore it? Would it happen again, this time with a different conclusion?

Hayley turned up the radio, focused on the traffic, and tried not to think about the small parcel in her purse—the one she'd ducked into the drugstore to buy during her lunch hour.

When she arrived home, Grant and Slim were on the pier cleaning fish, while Slim's dog and Bluster rough-and-tumbled in the grass nearby. The men waved a hearty greeting as she approached, and Bluster ran over to be petted.

"You're just in time," Grant said. "We've just about got these filleted, and I'm grilling them for dinner."

"If that's an invitation, I accept," Hayley replied. "Did you catch those yourselves?"

Slim cursed benignly and winked at Grant. "Now, isn't that just like a woman? We're knocking ourselves out in that boat for hours to bring home something for supper, and she wants to know if we caught them ourselves."

"In the hot sun," Grant chimed in. "On those hard seats. Baiting those hooks, and casting and casting and—"

"You two are breaking my heart!" Hayley said, laughing.

"It's the one question you never ask a fisherman," Grant explained.

"Well, pardon me," Hayley said. "What kind are they, anyway?"

"Bass, mostly," Slim said. "There's one good-size catfish. I thought I'd take it over to my daughter, let her fry it up for that brood of hers. Those kids'll be on it faster than a duck on a June bug."

He pointed his fillet knife toward the dogs. "Your pup had himself a merry time today."

"You took Bluster in the boat with you?" Hayley asked, surprised.

"Didn't occur to me you'd mind," Grant said.

"I don't. I just can't imagine him in a boat."

"He had to smell everything from stern to bow," Slim admitted.

"He *loved* the bait bucket," Grant interjected.

Hayley wrinkled her nose at the thought of dead, smelly bait. "I'll bet."

"Like father, like son," Slim said. "He took to it like a born sailor." He knelt at the edge of the pier and swished the knife in the water to clean it. "Grant tells me you want to get started on that dog run. If you'll show me where you want it, I'll take measurements and get it up tomorrow."

"Great!" Hayley said. "I can show you now, if you like. I was going to the house anyway."

She looked at Grant. "I'd like to get out of these clothes and into something more comfortable."

She hadn't realized how suggestive the cliché would sound until she saw the look of smug male camaraderie Slim shot Grant. "Can I bring something for dinner?" she asked, ignoring the byplay. "A salad, or veggies?"

"All contributions welcome," Grant said. "I hadn't thought much beyond the fish. If you have some potatoes, we could bake them in the coals."

Hayley nodded. "I'll get them. And toss a salad." She turned to Slim, who'd finished wrapping the catfish and stepped into the boat to put them in his ice chest. "Ready?"

"Just let me get my tape measure." He foraged through an ancient-looking metal toolbox until he found it, then hopped back onto the pier. "Those gardenias sure smell sweet," he commented, as they passed the copse of bushes.

"It's almost like having a park right outside the door," Hayley agreed.

"This whole place is like that. When we first moved in, I used to go to the window every morning, just to see for myself that the lake was there. Martha used to get real amused at me." A shadow passed over his eyes at the mention of his wife.

"When did she—?"

"Die? About three years ago."

"You must miss her very much."

"We were married thirty-seven years." Lost in thought, he stared down at the tape measure in his hands as though wondering what it was. "It's the little things, you know. You miss the little things." He exhaled a long breath. "That woman sure knew how to fry up a catfish."

"I've never heard a woman praised so highly," Hayley said, with a gentle smile.

Slim smiled back. "Now. Just where'd you want that dog run?"

After a bit of deliberation, they decided on a location and approximate size. While he measured, Hayley said, "I'd like to know more about Arthur Ramsey and his daughter. I tried the library, but they don't have high school yearbooks, and the school's old annuals were destroyed in a flooded storage room back in the sixties. Do you think there might be someone in town who knew them?"

He gave her an indulgent man-to-woman-with-a-whim look. "Beefing up on the local history, huh?"

"Just curious. Arthur Ramsey built my house."

"There should be somebody around who knew them. I've got to pick up the fencing at the hardware store. I'll ask Charlie Walters. If anybody knows, he'd be the one. He's been here forever and knows everybody."

"Great!"

"Seems to me someone said the girl's name was Cynthia," he told her, reeling his metal carpenter's tape from its holder. It didn't take him long to measure the area and estimate the cost of the fencing. Hayley wrote him a check, then went inside to change her clothes. The master bedroom was the only room in the house with wall-to-wall carpeting, and Hayley had wondered at Agnes O'Keefe's decision to cover the beautiful hardwood floors that added so much warmth to the other rooms. But it was pure pleasure to feel her stocking feet sink into the plush, rose-colored broadloom when she stepped out of her shoes.

She was just buttoning up the camp shirt she'd picked out to go with her khaki city shorts when a sharp crackling sound startled her. She spun round, then sighed in relief when she discovered that the racket had been nothing more ominous than the bedroom door slamming shut.

Funny, she thought, as she started across the room to reopen it, *it's never done that before.* Still, drafts and unusual air currents were not uncommon in old, high-ceilinged houses. Probably something in the combination of windows she'd opened and ceiling fans she'd turned on had created just the necessary flow to suck the door closed.

But not to turn the key in the lock. Hayley froze at the sound of old tumblers clunking into place. The weight of fear settled in her chest. Except for the modern dead-bolt locks on the exterior doors, the locks throughout the house were the old-fashioned type that took long keys with ornate heads. Had she routinely closed and locked her bedroom door, the key would have been on the interior side; since she normally left it open, the lovely old key was kept where it was visible when the door was open—the side that faced the hall when it was closed.

She took a breath to steady her nerves. The vibration of the door hitting the jamb had probably jarred the tumblers. She might be able to jiggle the knob and coax the door open.

But as she reached for the knob, she was overwhelmed by the sensation of a presence on the other side of that slab of wood. She was not alone in the house. The knowledge came to her with the certainty of death. Someone—or something—was on the other side of that door. She grabbed the knob and worked it back and forth, futilely. "Who's there?"

Dead silence.

"Grant? Grant, if you're out there, this isn't funny."

Succumbing to panic, Hayley pummeled the wood with her fist and shouted, "Unlock this door this minute! Do you hear me?" Her panic spent, she added in a whimper, "Grant?"

"You won't be seeing him tonight."

The voice, all too familiar, thundered through the door and echoed off the papered and wainscoted walls. Hayley was terrified. And furious. This couldn't be happening! It was like a scene from a corny old B movie where someone gets locked in the attic and slowly starves to death. Hayley drew in a ragged breath. "Wanta bet?" she cried through the door.

She wasn't in a movie and she wasn't in an attic, and she certainly wasn't going to starve to death when there was a window she could crawl out of and a big, brawny neighbor less than a football field's length from her.

She continued her tirade. "No puffed-up bag of ectoplasm is going to bully me, do you hear me?"

"Slut! Tramp!"

"Why don't you learn some new words, huh? Why don't you just...dissolve...or something? Just go away, and leave me alone!" She tried the door again, with no success.

"You won't go out flirting and carrying on like a whore tonight!" Arthur growled.

"I'll go anywhere I damned well want to go, you old fogy. I'm not your daughter!" Hayley felt the wetness of tears on her cheeks as she thought of her father, so amiable and gentle-natured—and so far away. More furious and frustrated than ever, she plopped down on the edge of the bed to compose herself. Gradually her heart quit pounding, her hands stopped shaking and she was able to think. She wiped the tears from her cheeks with her fingertips, walked resolutely to the window that overlooked the lake and raised it.

Half expecting it to slam back shut, she stepped away from it a moment, then laughed at herself. Just to be on the safe side, however, she took the tallest book of several on the bedside table and wedged it between the window and the sill before putting her hand under the window to test the screen.

The screen didn't yield when she gave it a shove, but there was nothing mysterious about that; large-headed nails held it in place, not ghostly fingers. Hayley paused and considered what to do. She didn't want to destroy the screen if she could help it. Grant was dumping charcoal into the fire bowl of a barbecue grill he'd set up on the patch of grass between the pier and the bait shop. She called out his name several times, but he didn't hear her. In desperation, she put the tips of two fingers in her mouth and let out the piercing whistle that she had once used to hail taxicabs in New York City.

Grant's head jerked around. This time he heard her cries and she managed to communicate that she wanted to talk to him. He put down the charcoal and jogged across the yard toward the house, with Bluster tagging along at his heels. When he was within easy earshot he asked, "Something wrong?"

"My door slammed shut. Think you can rescue me?"

"Damsels in distress are my specialty," he said drolly. "How do I find the right room?"

"There's only one hallway. Find the door that's locked."

He bowed deeply, like a Shakespearean player. "Your wish is my command."

Hayley grinned. The fishing trip has been therapeutic; whimsical humor was a side of him that was new to her. She watched until she could no longer see him, then waited in the middle of the room, listening for his footsteps.

An awful thought struck her: What if Arthur had locked the outside doors? What if he became violent? So far, he'd been more annoying than threatening, but he thought Hayley was his daughter. What if he mistook Grant for his daughter's suitor? Would he be as benign to him?

Hayley's knees went weak at the thought that she might have lured Grant into a perilous situation. The sound of his footsteps in the hallway a few seconds later was immensely reassuring.

The doorknob jiggled. "Hayley?"

"Grant?"

"No. It's the bogeyman!" Grant's acerbic reply was reassuringly typical of him. "Where's the key?"

"What do you mean, where's the key? It's in the lock." In a voice filled with long-suffering male patience, he replied, "If the key was in the lock, I'd have opened the door by now."

So old Arthur was getting wily, stealing keys, Hayley thought. He must have a streak of the poltergeist in him. "It must have fallen out when the door slammed shut. Look around for it."

"It's not anywhere within bouncing distance," Grant reported.

"Are you sure?"

"I've got a bloodhound with me. Trust me, Hayley, if there was a key here, he'd have tracked it down. His nose has been going ninety to nothing."

So Arthur was gone; otherwise, Bluster would be howling his head off, Hayley thought. Relief poured through her. "Get a key from another door," she suggested. "There should be one in the next bedroom."

"Will it fit the lock?"

"We won't know until you try it, will we?" She crossed her fingers for luck, hoping that Arthur hadn't pilfered the keys from the adjoining rooms.

Seconds later she heard a key click in the old lock. There was a creak, then the mechanical thunks of the old tumblers yielding. Grant's grin was the first thing Hayley saw as the door opened. "Your standard hero's welcome will suffice," he said.

Hayley felt like rushing into his arms and begging him never to let her go, but as Grant stepped into the doorway, she was filled with a sensation of foreboding so powerful that she froze, unable to move.

He was in genuine danger. She felt it in every fiber of her body. If he came into that room, something awful would happen. Something violent. Something terrible beyond imagining. She felt cold, as though all the blood had suddenly drained from her limbs.

"You can't come in here!" she snapped.

Grant raised his eyebrows playfully. "Afraid I'll compromise you?"

"I mean it, Grant!" She stepped in front of him, blocking him. "I...left my underwear out on the bed."

He chuckled, leaned to one side and peered past her into the room. "Oh? What color are they?"

Frustration blended with panic. Old Sourpuss had picked one hell of a time to locate his long-lost sense of humor. She couldn't explain this peculiar feeling; if she tried, he'd think she was one egg short of a dozen. There was no time for explanations, anyway. She had to get him out of that room. Away from— She didn't know what, only that the threat of danger was very real.

Luckily Bluster sensed it, too, and his howl distracted Grant enough for Hayley to nudge him out of the room. While he knelt to comfort the puppy, she closed the door and heaved a sigh of relief when she heard the latch click into place.

Cradling Bluster in his arms, Grant rose, and Hayley looped her elbow around his and shepherded him down the hall. "Come on. You can show me how to prepare the potatoes."

Grant selected two potatoes and showed her how to wet them and wrap them in foil for cooking in the coals. Then he sliced vegetables for the salad while Hayley washed the lettuce.

"You're pretty handy in the kitchen," Hayley commented, as Grant scraped cucumber disks from the cutting board into the salad bowl.

Grant put down the knife, and stepping behind Hayley, slipped his arms around her waist and kissed the area where her neck met her shoulder. "Think so?"

The effect on Hayley's senses was electric. Still shaky from the unsettling experience in the bedroom, she gasped softly in surprise.

"You're tense," he murmured.

"I didn't get much—" she found it hard to concentrate as he sprinkled her neck with tiny kisses "—sleep last night."

Gradually the tension in her body eased and she let her shoulders relax into the seductive warmth of his chest. Grant tightened his arms around her waist. "What happened to my hero's kiss?"

He nibbled the back of her neck and sent tremors of desire tingling along her nerve endings, all the way to her womb. Hayley bowed her head forward and moaned softly.

"Turn around and kiss me," he whispered, his breath hot and moist on her cheek. Hayley gladly obliged and melted against him where their bodies touched.

Grant's mouth fused over hers, his lips pliant and persuasive. After Arthur Ramsey's shenanigans and the disturbing foreboding of violence, she welcomed the oblivion that the kiss provided; the reassurance of a warm male body next to hers; the solace of having strong, caring arms around her.

He seemed to sense her need for human contact, and held her long after ending the kiss. Several minutes passed before he said, sounding regretful, "If I don't get the charcoal lit, it'll be midnight before dinner's ready."

Hayley lifted her cheek from his chest and tilted her head back to look at him. "How long does it take to grill food?"

The question amused Grant. "City girl, huh?"

Hayley shrugged her shoulders. "No balconies in our building."

"It'll take about half an hour to get the coals going enough to put in the potatoes. They'll take about an hour. The fish won't take any time at all. That reminds me—you wouldn't happen to have a lemon, would you?"

"I have some frozen lemon juice."

"That'll work. Lemon juice and melted butter make the best basting sauce."

"I'll mix some up after I finish the salad."

Grant leaned forward and kissed the tip of her nose. "Give it a healthy dash of pepper."

They ate on the bait shop porch, sitting in the rocking chairs with their plates on their laps, with only the moon, the glow of the briquets in the grill and the citronella candle for light.

"What do you think?" Grant asked, as Hayley took her first bite of grilled fish.

"You could never do *this* in a microwave," she replied wryly.

Grant cast her a grimace of mock disgust. "Nuke a fish? Bite your tongue, woman!"

"It really was excellent," Hayley said, a few minutes later, as Grant took her empty plate. He carried the plates into the shop and returned with two small waxed-paper-wrapped packages, one of which he dropped in Hayley's lap. "What's this?" she asked.

"Dessert," he explained. "The Moon Pies I ordered for Slim came in."

"Moon Pies?"

"Don't tell me you've never had one of these, either."

"Okay. I won't tell you."

"You haven't!"

She raised her eyebrows.

"We'll make a Southerner of you yet," he said confidently. He'd finished his pie by the time she'd opened hers. He watched her examine the chocolate-dipped cookie-and-marshmallow sandwich curiously and take her first bite, then asked, "What d'you think?"

"It must be an acquired taste." She put the cookie back in the package and set it on the table between the chairs.

Grant laughed. "Only for Yankees." He picked up the package. "Do you mind?"

"Be my guest."

"I haven't had a Moon Pie in at least ten years," he said, taking the pie from the wrapper.

They rocked awhile; the squeaking of the rocker rails on the wooden porch added to the night symphony of frogs, insects and slapping water. The scents of citronella and gardenia hung in the moist night air.

Ironically, it was the peace of the moment that forced Hayley to reflect on the troubling events of the afternoon. While they were preparing dinner and Grant was teaching her the finer points of charcoal cooking, she'd managed to avoid thinking about the significance of being locked in her room by a curmudgeon of a ghost. She'd successfully put off remembering the queer sense of foreboding that had sent her into a panic. Now, the memory of standing in her room, terrified for Grant's safety, came to her with a clarity that made her hands clammy and her chest tight.

She was cold, too. Her cheeks. Her ears. Her bare legs. The rocker was large, the seat wide and deep. She drew her legs up, hugged her knees and tilted her head to rest her cheek on top of them. What had happened to the paradise she'd left New York for? To the independence she had flaunted with so much confidence?

A ghost, that's what.

A ghost! Other people grew up, left home, became independent. They worried about making mortgage payments. They got lonely. They had the normal adjustments to make. But they didn't have ghosts who called them names and locked them in their rooms. They didn't have strange forebodings of violence that left them shaken. Why her? Why did she have to be the one?

Vaguely aware that Grant had spoken, she lifted her head.

"What's wrong, Hayley?"

"There's no one . . . to talk to." She stared at him blankly, scarcely hearing her own words. "If I tell anyone, they'll think I'm crazy."

"You can tell me," he said.

Her gaze met his. "You'll think I'm crazy, too."

Grant shrugged. "Turnabout is fair play."

"I don't know what you mean." She couldn't concentrate.

"You suggested I go to a shrink, remember?"

Hayley inhaled deeply and exhaled slowly. "That's different. You'd just need a little help in adjusting. They'd slap a straitjacket on me and put me in a padded room."

"Hayley, for God's sake—what's got you so upset?"

She didn't answer. After a pause, he persisted. "Does this have anything to do with why you wouldn't let me in your bedroom?"

She looked at him for a long moment before she finally asked, "Do you think that chair would support two people?"

"Let's find out," he said, and spread his arms in invitation.

She curled up in his lap and laid her head on his shoulder while he wrapped his arms around her and rocked the chair in a lazy motion. A sigh came from deep inside her, and she snuggled more closely against him. She breathed in the scent of his after-shave. His hard male body, warm and vital and reassuringly human, warmed her.

"It wasn't because you had underwear strewn over the bed, was it?" he asked gently.

Hayley's fingers curled around a handful of his shirt, bunched it into her fist and held it tight. It anchored her to the reassurance his presence offered. "No," she answered mournfully.

He pulled her closer, and cradled her head against him with his hand. "You're trembling. God, Hayley, what's wrong?"

Hayley didn't know how to tell him, where to start. How did one explain the inexplicable? She said, simply, "My door didn't just slam shut and lock all by itself."

"Someone deliberately locked you in?" Her cheek rubbed against the hollow of his shoulder as she nodded affirmatively. Grant didn't like seeing her so upset—and the idea of someone bothering her stirred every protective instinct in him. "Who would do that? And why?"

"He wanted to . . . keep me away from you."

His blood boiled at the idea of an ex-boyfriend bullying her, intimidating her. "Is someone harassing you?"

"Sort of."

"He was in your room, wasn't he? Hayley, if someone's threatening you, you don't have to put up with it. You can get legal help. A restraining order, or—"

"I can't get a restraining order against Arthur Ramsey."

7

"ARTHUR RAMSEY?" It took a moment for the name to register with Grant, and when it did, it made no sense. "The man who built your house? But he's—"

"Dead," Hayley finished for him.

If she hadn't been so upset he might have thought she was kidding. But she was serious—dead serious—and sad.

"He's a ghost," she said, then swallowed. "And he's haunting my house."

Her distress was very real. She actually believed it, and it was tearing her apart. "Just because a door slammed shut—"

"It wasn't just the door," she continued, sounding so resigned that Grant's heart ached for her. "That wasn't the first time I've seen him. Or heard him."

"He talks to you?" *It was worse than he'd realized.*

"He—mostly, he calls me names."

Despite his skepticism, Grant found her wild story morbidly fascinating. "What kind of names?"

She drew a deep breath. "'Tramp' and 'slut' are his favorites. Names your typical overbearing father might have called a rebellious daughter in the forties." She lifted her head and met his gaze evenly. "He thinks I'm his daughter, Cynthia."

She really believes it, Grant thought. *She's convinced her house is haunted.* It was probably a simple case of an overactive imagination fed by circumstances. Or she could be stark, raving mad. Either way, she was genuinely upset. "Hayley—"

"You don't believe me, do you? About Arthur Ramsey."

"I believe that you believe Arthur Ramsey is haunting your house."

With a dismal sigh, she lowered her head to his shoulder again. "I knew you'd think I was crazy."

"I didn't say that."

"Not in so many words."

"Hayley—"

Her head came up. "Don't 'Hayley' me in that patronizing tone. Either my house is haunted, and I'm sane, or it's not haunted and I'm hallucinating. It's obvious which interpretation you favor."

"You've got to admit that the idea of a ghost is a little startling. If you didn't think so, you wouldn't be afraid everyone might think you were crazy for talking about it."

Her shoulders sagged as she pressed her forehead against his temple. "If I told the people at work...I don't know what they'd do. I called my mother, but I couldn't just...blurt out that the marvelous house I've been raving about is haunted."

It had never occurred to him how isolated she was. Every time he'd seen her she'd been friendly and vivacious; he'd always imagined her surrounded by people at work, and assumed that she had a full social life, as well. But now that he tried, he couldn't remember anyone visiting her. Nor did he recall her traipsing out to her car dressed to the nines for a night on the town.

All of which added credibility to the theory that she might create a ghost to help fill the gap that her family had always filled in her life—and all of which meant that if he allowed himself to be pulled into the role of her sole confidant he was in for a lot more than a friendly good-morning nod and some puppy-sitting.

His jaw set as he contemplated the situation he was in. Becoming the steadfast friend of a lonely young woman with an overactive imagination was not what he'd had in mind when he'd defected from the rat race. He didn't want the responsibility, the moral obligation. And yet—

She was in his lap, clinging to him, needing him. And her need was seductive.

Grant couldn't remember the last time anyone had actually *needed* him. The good old U.S. of A. had *needed* him, but that wasn't the same thing. That had been an impersonal need for troop strength calculated by generals and military advisers. He'd merely been one among the thousands. Hundreds of thousands.

Melissa hadn't needed him, had never needed him; had made a point of declaring that fact at every opportunity. Eventually, not to need each other had become a crazy competition and was one of the things that had undermined their relationship and doomed it to

failure. What was a partnership without mutual need
as well as mutual understanding and support?

Partnership. Relationship. Both required mutual
need. But he wasn't in the market for either—or, at
least, he *hadn't* been when he'd walked off the job and
out of his former life. He'd wanted a clean break, iso-
lation, time for contemplation, freedom from responsibility, room to discover what kind of life he wanted.
If he had any notion of holding on to what he'd come
searching for, his wisest move would be to tell Hayley
she had bats in her belfry and bounce her off his lap
onto her cute little behind.

Thinking of her cute little bottom was a mistake. He
was suddenly acutely aware of the pleasurable weight
of her buttocks on his thighs. And once aware of her
bottom on his thighs, he found it impossible not to notice her forehead against his temple, her breath fan-
ning his cheek, her hair tickling his nose and her left
breast crushed against his chest.

His sudden desire for her made him feel slightly dis-
honorable. She had trusted him enough to curl up in his
lap and confide in him. Her appeal for understanding
and trust was almost childlike in its directness and simplicity. He'd never seen anyone as vulnerable. And he'd
never wanted so desperately to comfort and protect
another human being.

He gave her a reassuring hug. "Tell me about the first
time you saw him."

"That was when . . . I didn't know he was a ghost. I
thought he was part of my—" She swallowed. "A dream

I had. The next time I was wide awake. It was the night you picked the gardenia. Do you remember—you kissed me?"

"I remember."

"I went inside and . . . suddenly he was there, glowering at me, and calling me names. I recognized him from the dream, but this time I wasn't dreaming, I was awake, and I couldn't believe . . . I was too scared to think, and Bluster was howling. You heard him this afternoon. He seems to sense— It's some kind of animal instinct, I guess. I couldn't think. I just reacted, and threw something at him."

Her arm tightened around his neck, and she burrowed her face in the crook where his neck and shoulder joined. "It went straight through him. That's when I knew what he was."

She raised her head and released her claw-like grip on his shirt. "I haven't seen him since then, but I've heard him whispering insults in my room at night. I . . . talk back to him, try to convince him that I'm not his daughter. I didn't think he had the ability to hurt me, but after today—"

Grant was almost totally convinced that she had made up the ghost, but before he gently suggested that idea to her, he wanted to know more about the phantom she had created. "Why do you think he has you confused with his daughter? Has he ever called you by her name?"

"No. It's— Don't you see? It's the emotion. Arthur Ramsey freaked out when his daughter got romantically involved with a man. When she left with her lover, he perceived it as a defection. It haunted him to his dying day, and it was unresolved when he died."

Grant couldn't keep the skepticism out of his voice. "Leaving him earthbound and restless."

"I'm probably about the age Cynthia was when she eloped. When I came in feeling... after you kissed me... it must have been like déjà vu to him."

"Feeling what?" he asked, touching her face with his fingertips; he couldn't seem to touch her enough.

She paused before answering. Tempestuous emotion roiled in the depths of her eyes when she raised her head to look at him. She released his shirt and let her hand rest on his shoulder. She spoke in a near whisper. "The way a woman feels when a man puts a flower in her hair and kisses her."

"Romantic?"

"Romantic, yes. And feminine. And—" she smiled "—desirable."

"Desirable enough to wake the dead?"

"*Desired* enough for Arthur Ramsey to tune in to the emotional state I was in."

"One kiss made you that emotional?"

"It wasn't just the kiss. It was everything. The moonlight. The gardenia. The way you looked at me. A woman knows when a man finds her desirable, Grant, especially when—"

"When?" Grant prompted gently.

"When she—"

"What?"

"Finds him—"

"Desirable?"

She grinned. "Attractive."

"So you came in all starry-eyed and mellow, and the emotions you were feeling roused the ghost of a man who's been dead for years."

"He was already...active. My dream—" She realized her mistake too late.

"You're blushing," he said.

"You couldn't possibly tell that—it's too dark."

"It's not that dark."

"I never blush."

"It's the second time you've mentioned your dream. Going to tell me about it?"

"Not in this lifetime."

"Must must have been a humdinger."

She remained exasperatingly silent. "X-rated?" he asked drolly.

"PG-13. Arthur Ramsey woke me up before it got too...explicit."

"Was I in it?"

"No!"

"Liar." He grinned devilishly. "Was I dressed?"

"In an elegant tuxedo."

"The whole time?"

"Yes."

"Were you dressed?"

"Yes. In something black and slinky."

"The whole time?"

She didn't answer.

"You're blushing again," he observed. Still, she didn't answer. He asked, "What'd we do to rattle Arthur Ramsey's bones?"

"*You* were the only one *doing* anything," she said. "I was merely enjoying what you were doing. And *that's* what got old Arthur whipped into a frenzy. One second you were kissing me, and the next thing I knew, Arthur Ramsey was calling me a tramp."

His grin became lascivious. "Did you kiss me back?"

She laughed softly—a throaty, sexy laugh. "That would have been physically impossible."

Suddenly Grant's throat was dry and tight, making his voice husky. "Where . . . was I . . . kissing you?"

Hayley drew up her right leg and braced her heel against the edge of the seat of the chair, bringing her knee within inches of his face. "Here." She pointed to her ankle. "And . . . here."

She touched the inside of her thigh, just above her knee. At first, all Grant could do was stare. Still winter pale, her skin was the color of rich cream and he had a strange notion that he could drink its pale, seductive smoothness.

He touched it first with his thumb, teasing its alabaster silkiness with the remnants of calluses developed in the desert. Her response was a provocative little gasp.

He forced his eyes away from her creamy thigh to search her face. The expression in her eyes reflected the desire he felt for her.

"Like this?" he whispered, and slowly lowered his mouth to her thigh. He'd never kissed a woman there, and that he should be doing so when they were both fully dressed was more arousing than if they were both naked. His entire consciousness focused on that expanse of skin. He tested its texture with his lips, tasted it with his tongue, teased it with his teeth, drew on its creamy softness with sucking kisses.

His body heavy and heated with wanting her, Grant raised his head and discovered the invitation he'd hoped to see in her eyes. As he fused his mouth over hers, her lips parted, inviting plunder. A sensual purr deep in her throat urged him on, as did the urgent, restless clawing of her hands on his back.

He dragged his mouth away from hers. His chest heaved as he looked into her face and wondered how to get her from the porch to a place of privacy.

She was the first to speak, her words soft and slurred by passion. "I went to the drugstore today."

He answered, with something akin to a chuckle, "So did I."

"You didn't have to tell me that," she said, dropping her forehead to his. "But I'm so glad you did."

Her mouth was too close, irresistibly close. He kissed her briefly. "My place—?" He gave her another quick kiss. "Or yours?"

She pondered the question a moment. "Yours."

"You sure?" he asked.

"I don't know what he'd do."

Grant frowned. "Arthur Ramsey?"

"Neither of us is in any mood to find out."

Grant couldn't have agreed more. He might not believe Arthur Ramsey existed outside her mind, but he wasn't going to argue the point. Philosophical debates over the existence of ghosts were not on his agenda for the next few hundred hours.

His body was so taut from wanting her he wasn't sure he'd be able to pull himself out of the rocker, but he did so easily enough when Hayley crawled off his lap, blew out the citronella candles and, reaching for his hand, turned to him with a come-hither smile.

Till the day he died, he would treasure that image of Hayley in the pale moonlight, reaching for him, offering herself to him. He took her hand and, with a courtliness he didn't know he was capable of, lifted it to his lips to kiss it before curling his fingers around hers.

"It's not fancy," he warned, when they reached the door that separated the shop from the storeroom that he had converted into living quarters.

"It's private."

"Or it will be," he said wryly, eyeing Bluster meaningfully. "I think it's time your doggie had some gourmet doggie biscuits—in the bathroom."

"I don't know how he'll react to being locked up."

"He'll be all right. I left him in there today when I went out. He might cry for a few minutes, but he can't hurt himself."

He dropped a kiss on Hayley's lips. "I don't want to share you with *anyone* right now. Not even a dog."

Hayley nodded. Grant's brief absence gave her just enough time to become self-conscious about being in his private living space, which was dominanted by the twin-size bed.

When Grant stepped out of the bathroom after putting out the doggie biscuits for Bluster he suddenly saw the room as Hayley must see it, a cubbyhole with a bed, chest of drawers, fishing posters on the wall and a bare light bulb in the center of the ceiling.

"Look around, Hayley," he said. "This is my life right now. It's all I have to offer." He paused. "It's not 'forever,' wrapped up in pretty pink ribbons."

She met his gaze unflinchingly. "I just moved out of my parents' home, Grant. I'm not looking for 'forever' wrapped up in pretty pink ribbons."

"In that case—" The cocky grin and smoldering look he gave her as he wrapped his arms around her would have ignited damp wood. "Why don't you kiss me."

Hayley was more than anxious to oblige. She kissed him lightly then slid her tongue over his bottom lip while she wove her hands into his hair and massaged his ears with her thumbs. Subtly, but decisively, she nudged her pelvic area against his.

Grant responded by opening his mouth and pulling her even closer to the center of his aching need. The sudden intimate contact with the rock-hard evidence of her effect on him surprised Hayley, then made her bold. She spread exploratory kisses all over his face— on his eyelids and along his jaw—and nipped his earlobe with her teeth.

Grant growled as she sucked on the tender skin beneath his ear. She bit him playfully. He reciprocated by pinching her behind. She gasped in surprise and slid her hands under his shirttail and grabbed a handful of the golden hair that furred his flat abdomen.

"Don't do it," he said, his voice sharp-edged with warning.

"What?" she asked. "This?" Opening her hands, she massaged him in ever-larger semicircles that soon had her palms teasing his nipples. Pushing his shirt up, she followed with her mouth, licking the dark circles with her tongue until their peaks were pebbled.

Grant shrugged out of his shirt and flung it aside, then reached for the top button of her shirt. "Turnabout is fair play."

Giggling, Hayley slapped his hands away. "No."

"Yes!" he insisted, a determined gleam in his eye.

"No!" Hayley returned in playful defiance.

"All right. Leave it on. We'll do it the hard way."

"Do wha—?" Before she could complete the word, she was in his iron embrace, being crushed solidly against his hard frame. He kissed her, not gently, and used his left arm as an anchor across her waist to hold her close. With his right hand, he cupped her breast, kneading its peak until the satin of her bra felt like burlap abrading her aroused flesh.

Her breasts grew heavy and hot, aching for the more intimate touch of skin against skin, but when he slipped his hand under her shirt, it was to splay his fingers over her back. He moved his mouth to her breast and nibbled and sucked through her shirt until the wet shirt and bra clung to her erect nipple like extra layers of skin.

"Grant," she pleaded, thrusting her chest upward in blatant invitation.

"Oh, no," he said. "We want the shirt *on*."

Smiling wickedly, she met and held his gaze. "Playing dirty, are we?"

She hooked her thumbs under the gathered waistband of her shorts and slowly slipped them past her hips and let them fall to the floor. "Now we're even—you've got bottoms, I've got a top."

Grant was mesmerized by the sight of her satiny panties with their sheer, peekaboo appliqués. The passion burning in the depths of his eyes and his labored breathing as he stared at her set her own pulse racing. She felt desirable, powerful, recklessly bold. Impulsively she turned her back to him and let him see her buttocks—bare except for the ridiculously small expanse of satin. She cast a coquettish look over her shoulder and wiggled her bottom from side to side. "Like what you see?"

"No."

Hayley turned to face him and they exchanged knowing smiles. "Too bad," she said, then slipped her hands around his waist to knead his buttocks. "I've always thought you had great buns. I was looking forward to seeing them."

Grant had not anticipated this side of Hayley's personality; the playful, beguiling seductress who now was brazenly sliding her knee up and down the length of his achingly hard erection. "You're killing me," he rasped.

Hayley moved her mouth away from the nipple she'd been torturing. "Too bad you have to die with your pants on. We could have had such fun."

Muttering an obscenity, Grant wrenched away from her and struggled with the hook above the zipper of his shorts. Hayley covered his hands and shook her head. "Uh-uh. Not while I still have my blouse on."

Repeating the expletive, Grant grabbed the vee where the lapels of her shirt came together, gave a savage yank and sent buttons flying in every direction.

"That was one of my best shirts!"

"Buy another just like it and send me the bill," Grant replied. His fingers drove her mad as he tried to figure out the catch of her bra. When it opened, he brushed aside the two triangular satin cups and shoved both bra straps and blouse off her shoulders.

Instantly his hands were on her breasts, kneading and chafing. Hayley moaned at the sensual assault and twined her arms around his neck. Grant lowered his mouth to her breast and she had to cling to him for support.

Hayley was convinced she had unleashed a demon as his hands moved over her flesh. Then he splayed them over her buttocks and jerked her forward and grated his pelvis against the depression between her thighs.

"Kiss me," she gasped.

It was an urgent kiss. Grant probed her mouth hungrily, as though he might consume her. Hayley tightened her arms around his neck and matched his ardor. She wrapped her legs around his hips and locked her ankles behind him.

Grant took stumbling steps backward and dropped onto the bed with Hayley in his lap, her bare breasts pressed against his chest, her legs still wrapped around him. He felt her hands slide between their bodies to work at his pants.

He lowered his gaze to watch, and gasped as her fingertips grazed his swollen shaft as she opened the zipper. "Don't stop now," he said.

The sight of her parted thighs and the strip of satin hiding the sweet, secret part of her that beckoned him was stimulating, but when she honored his request and caressed him through his knit briefs, he felt he might burst with the pure pleasure of it.

He wrapped his arms tightly around her and fell back on the bed, pulling her, still astride him, with him.

"Hayley," he whispered, kissing her neck, her jaw, her eyelids. "Beautiful . . . Hayley."

"Hmmm," Hayley murmured. "Nice." He was still kissing her, discovering sensitive little places that had never known a man's adoring attention. Still touching, kissing, he removed her panties.

"I want—" she whimpered.

"What?"

"That," she told him, arching against him as he probed her warm, wet recesses with his fingers. She gasped loudly and shuddered as the heel of his hand swept across her sensitive mound.

"You're ready for me," he said, awed by her response to his touch. "I'm just as desperate for you," he whispered in her ear.

She groaned in protest when he rolled away to take off his jeans. Standing at the bed's edge, he searched his front pocket for the foil pouch he'd stuffed in it while in the bathroom, then shoved his pants and briefs down his legs.

His back was to the bed. Sensing her gaze on him, he glanced back over his shoulder at Hayley and grinned. "Like what you see?"

"No," Hayley lied. His buttocks were firm and fit and beautifully muscled.

"Too bad," Grant replied. "I was going to let you touch them."

"I might touch them even if they're not pretty."

"Is that a promise?" He got back into bed, and pulled her into his arms. She sighed as her breasts compressed against his chest, and their legs entwined.

"It's different without denim," she mused dreamily.

"Better?" he asked.

"It just keeps getting better."

His mouth met hers for a deep kiss, while she swept her hands down the sleek muscles of his back to test the firmness of his buns. Grant broke the kiss with a sigh. "Still ready for me?"

"Mmm-hmm," she said, shifting her body to accommodate his.

"I'd have died from the wanting if you'd said no," he said. He was inside her immediately, overwhelmed by the sensation of belonging as her body encased him with velvety warmth.

She moved restlessly beneath him, and he responded with a thrust that drove him deeper inside her. She participated in their lovemaking in her own unique way, with unexpected touches, soft and urgent. Most surprising of all, she spoke to him in a sensual whisper, with words of praise and encouragement, expressing the pleasure he gave her. And when all the tension they'd built up exploded inside her and she clung to him with the force of a woman falling over a precipice, she called out his name.

The sound of it on her lips echoed in his mind as he tumbled over the precipice with her, and all he could say as he held her afterward and stroked her face with his fingertips was, "Hayley."

She snuggled against him. "Hmm."

There were many things he could have said, if he'd wanted to think. But he didn't want to think. He was afraid he might start analyzing why Hayley felt different in his arms than any woman he'd ever held. So he just indulged in the pleasure of holding her, and didn't say anything at all.

The peace of the moment was shattered by a series of thunks against the bathroom door, accompanied by the indignant yodels of a puppy too long ignored. "He won't give up if he knows we're here," Hayley warned.

"I've got to make a pit stop, anyway," Grant said and rolled to the edge of the bed.

Hayley watched him cross the room, and wolf-whistled as he reached for the bathroom door. Grant gave her an over-the-shoulder grin. "Thought you didn't like my buns."

"They're not so bad once you get used to them."

"Yeah. I think I could get used to yours, too."

She threw the pillow at him. Grant ducked successfully, then, laughing, opened the door.

When he returned from the bathroom, Hayley was sitting up in the bed, the sheet tucked under her arms, her back braced against a faded fishing poster on the wall behind the bed. Bluster was next to her, his head tossed back in ecstasy as she scratched his neck. Grant picked up the pillow Hayley had thrown at him and carried it to the bed. "You might be more comfortable with this."

"Thanks," she said, leaning forward so he could put it behind her shoulders. "Oh, and I want a shirt, too."

"A shirt?"

"Mine's next to useless," she reminded him with a wry smile. "The least you could do is give me a loaner to wear home."

"Home?"

"Home. My home. You've probably seen it. It's the little white frame house between here and the road."

Grant frowned as he opened a drawer to sift through the stack of shirts. "I was hoping you'd stay."

"I will, for a while." She picked up the white knit undershirt he tossed in her lap and put it on.

Grant climbed into bed next to her and spread one arm behind her head. With his free hand, he guided her face toward his and kissed her briefly on the lips. The bed was narrow enough to crowd two people, but seemed even narrower with a dog between them. Bluster, sensing a new source of affection, promptly planted his front paws on Grant's chest and licked his chin.

"Damned mutt," Grant grumbled. He grabbed the puppy by the scruff of the neck and carefully set him on the floor. "You shouldn't allow him on the bed. It's bad training."

"I didn't, until the other night, after Arthur . . . It felt pretty good to have a friend, you know. Even a hairy one."

He felt her involuntary shiver and urged her closer. She snuggled up against him and settled her head in the hollow of his shoulder. He kissed the top of her head. "Next time you need a friend—"

The end of the sentence was left hanging when Bluster lunged back onto the bed, landed on Grant's abdomen and walked on large, clumsy puppy feet down Grant's legs until he found a comfortable hollow between Grant's ankles and Hayley's.

"Do you suppose this is what parenthood is like?" Hayley asked.

"If so, it's a great recommendation for birth control."

"You don't like my dog?"

"I don't want to share you right now." He bent his knee and draped his leg over her thighs, then kissed the top of her head again. "You aren't really going to leave me tonight, are you?"

"I have to work in the morning, Grant."

He stroked his hand over the length of her arm. "So? Go home in the morning."

"Grant."

"Does this have anything to do with what you said earlier, about having just moved out of your parents' house?"

"A little. Mostly, it's just common sense. This bed isn't big enough to sleep two comfortably."

"I'm not uncomfortable, are you?"

"We're not exactly *sleeping*."

Grant was nibbling on her ear. "If you don't like my bed, we could try yours."

"No!"

Grant felt tension take hold of her body. The ghost again. He might not believe it was real, but it was certainly real to her. Either way, a dead man was coming between them, and Grant didn't like it one bit. "Does this have anything to do with the way you hustled me out of your bedroom this afternoon?"

Her silence was answer enough. He persisted. "What happened, Hayley?"

Hayley sighed wearily. "I'm not sure I can explain it."

"Give it a try."

She did, trying futilely to describe the sensation of imminent peril. "It sounds . . . lame, I know. But it was real, Grant. If you'd gone into that room, I don't know what would have happened."

"We could call his bluff."

"No! I won't be responsible."

"You're terrified for me to go into that room, and you expect me to let you go in there alone?"

"I don't expect you to *let* me do anything, Grant. It's my choice. Arthur Ramsey thinks I'm his daughter. He's irritating and a bit frightening, but no real threat to me. It's different with you. If he has me confused with Cynthia, he probably has you confused with the man she eloped with. For all I know, he may have been storing up his cosmic energy in order to punish his son-in-law."

"Cosmic energy?"

"Or ectoplasm, or whatever it is that ghosts use."

A grave silence followed.

Hayley knew her story sounded far fetched, and that Grant didn't believe her, but she hadn't the slightest doubt that Arthur Ramsey's ghost was haunting her house and harbored malevolent, possibly dangerous feelings toward Grant. She had to make him accept the reality of that menace.

Grant didn't believe for a moment that Hayley's house was haunted, but he wanted to put the issue of Arthur Ramsey's ghost to rest without destroying his developing relationship with Hayley. He had to make her accept the fact that there was no ghost.

But how? he mused. With great tact and diplomacy, obviously. But was there a tactful way to suggest that she was the victim of her own imagination without insulting her?

After several minutes of thoughtful silence, he said, "Were your parents strict, Hayley?"

"Not really," Hayley replied, obviously surprised by the question. "I was the youngest of three, so they were pretty much shockproof by the time I came along. According to my brother and sister, they were too lenient with me. Why?"

"You mentioned earlier that you had moved away from your parents' home for the first time. It seems to be an issue with you. I thought maybe they were strict disciplinarians."

"I'd probably have moved out a year or two sooner if that were the case."

"So why is it a big deal?"

"Moving away from home is always a big deal. Don't you remember the first time you moved out?"

"College dormitory room," he said, smiling nostalgically.

Hayley grinned. "See. I commuted to college, so I never lived on campus. And when I got my first job after graduation, I wasn't making enough to have my own place. Besides, every time I talked about moving out, my parents pointed out that I had my own room, and the price was right, so I just stayed. It was hard for them to let me go, since I was the baby of the bunch. When the company moved its headquarters and I saw the chance to make the break without it seeming like a defection, I jumped at it."

"They babied you?"

"I said I was the baby, not that they babied me. Why is this so important to you?"

"It's just . . . it seemed so important to you."

"Well, it's a big change. Moving into a house instead of an apartment. And not having to answer to anyone."

Ah! thought Grant. *The crux of the matter.* "I thought you said they weren't strict."

"They weren't. But when you live with other people, there are certain obligations. If I was going to miss a meal, I tried to let mother know, and I didn't just . . . not show up at night."

"And boyfriends?"

"Well, I didn't invite them in for cocktails and 'slip into something more comfortable,' if that's what you mean."

"That's what I meant. It must have been a little restrictive for you."

She shrugged. "I had to be discreet."

He kissed her forehead. "And now you don't have to be discreet anymore."

She smiled. "Let's just say that I can go home tonight wearing a man's T-shirt and carrying a buttonless blouse and not have to feel self-conscious." The smile faded. "I just hope Arthur Ramsey doesn't sense what I've been up to and hassle me."

"Maybe you like being hassled."

She looked at him as though he were nuts. "Like it?"

"Your parents aren't here to keep tabs on you. Maybe it's reassuring to have Arthur Ramsey keeping his eye on you."

Finally grasping his insinuation, she pushed up on one elbow and glared down at him. "You think I'm making Arthur Ramsey up?"

Her chest heaved as she glowered at him and her breasts swaying under the soft knit of his shirt reminded him that she was wearing no underwear at all. Her hair was mussed from their lovemaking and her cheeks flushed with fury. "I think you're the sexiest woman I've ever had the good fortune to share a bed with," he said, and raised his mouth to hers.

She pushed him away before he could kiss her. "Of all the things you could have said, that was probably the dumbest."

"Hayley."

He looked properly mortified, but that didn't defuse her anger. "You can't insinuate that I'm making up a ghost to replace my parents in one breath and try to flatter me out of being insulted the next. I don't know which is the more insulting of the two."

"I wasn't insulting you. I was complimenting you."

"What? It turns you on to think that a woman is so insecure and homesick that she'd manufacture a ghost to call her names and harass her about carnal thoughts because she doesn't have her parents around to put her on a guilt trip?"

With a lightning-swift movement, he rolled on top of her and pinned her to the mattress. "I'll tell you what turns me on! It's the way you look at me. The way you respond to me. The way you aren't afraid to let me know that you like me touching you. The way you aren't afraid to touch me. The way you sigh and wiggle and breathe under me. With all due respect, Ms. Addison, I love you in spite of your damned ghost, not because of him."

They stared at each other in total consternation, then spoke at the same time.

"Love?"

"Good God!"

There was a shocked silence. Then Grant gave a defeated groan. "Well, that explains a lot, doesn't it?"

"Like what?" Hayley asked, with rare timidity.

"Like why sex with you was better than my first roller-coaster ride. Like why I don't want you to go home. Like why I went flying out of here like an avenging warrior the other night when I thought you were in trouble. Like why having you under me, wearing nothing but my shirt is making me hard as a fifteen-year-old doing his first slow dance." He grimaced. "Like why I haven't *killed* the dog who's walking up my body with razor blades strapped to his clutzy paws."

"Bluster!" Hayley exclaimed, reaching around Grant to push the puppy away. He landed on the floor with a plop. "Is he hurt?" she asked, her eyes wide with fear.

"Take my word for it, the mutt's indestructible," Grant said, as he leaned forward to kiss her.

Neither noticed when the dog rejoined them on the bed, but Grant escorted the pup on a one-way trip to the bathroom when he paid a visit to the medicine chest a few minutes later.

An hour later the animal followed the two humans as Grant, voicing vehement objections, walked Hayley to her house and kissed her good-night on the front porch. She was still in his arms when he said, "I'm a fool to let you go into this house alone."

"It's not a matter of your 'letting' me do anything, Grant. I'm a big girl. I make my own decisions. I don't know what you're worried about, anyway. You don't even believe there *is* a ghost."

"I believe that you believe it. It's not healthy."

"Please don't remind me how furious I should be with you just when I'm about to go inside and dream about you."

"You're not going to change your mind, are you? About staying with me tonight or going in and calling Arthur Ramsey's bluff?"

"No. And, no."

"Promise you'll call if you need me. For any reason."

Hayley nodded. She stepped away from him and said, with an inarguable note of finality, "Good night, Grant."

Grant grumbled good-night and started down her walk. When she called his name, he turned hopefully, thinking that perhaps she'd changed her mind. But she said, "It's easy not to believe in ghosts until you've seen one."

They were at an impasse. Grant shoved his hands in his back pockets and frowned in frustration and displeasure over the entire situation. Finally, he turned and continued down the walk.

Hayley waited until he'd rounded the corner of the house before going inside. Both sated and tired, she wanted to take a leisurely hot bath and crawl straight into bed. She hoped Arthur Ramsey wouldn't tune in to her frame of mind and decide to make an appearance. It was too late and she had too many sweet moments with Grant to think about to put up with any of his ectoplasmic nonsense tonight.

She needn't have worried.

Arthur Ramsey wasn't waiting up for her. His daughter Cynthia was.

8

HAYLEY HAD BEEN IN the bathtub for almost half an hour when she sensed another presence in the room. At first, it was just a prickle of sensation, an awareness that something was not quite right, as if the room and everything in it were holding its breath. Despite the warmth of the water that surrounded her, Hayley shivered. She had put scented bath oil in the tub, but suddenly the scent of the gardenias blooming outside was stronger, almost cloying.

Now wary and alert, she raised her head from the curled rim of the tub. The presence appeared like a gentle whirlwind, spinning into shape before her astonished eyes, diaphanous yet distinctly human, distinctly feminine.

"Cynthia?" Hayley whispered. "It's you, isn't it?"

The words that came back to her were also whispered, and echoed strangely. "Warn him."

"Warn who?"

"He's watch-ing. Watch-ing." The oddly-cadenced words were muted, as though they came from far away. Already the whirlwind was spinning more slowly, losing the form that suggested a human being.

"Cynthia, don't go! Who am I supposed to warn? Is it Grant? Is he in danger?"

The whirlwind had lost all human shape. Translucent and ill-defined, it blew across the narrow room, and as it moved, the room seemed to come alive. The curtains fluttered and the door to the bottom section of the built-in shelving sprang open with a snap. Then, with a crash of paws against wood and the squeak of old hinges, Bluster pushed the bathroom door open, charged inside, and started to whine. The fluted glass bottle of bath oil that had been sitting next to the tub toppled and rolled across the floor. As it hit the side of the open cabinet, the ornate cork-lined stopper became dislodged and oil poured onto the floor; its heavy floral aroma filled the room.

And then, suddenly, all was quiet. The curtains no longer fluttered, the bottle no longer rolled, doors no longer moved with creaks and squeaks. Even Bluster, who had sat down in the middle of the floor, was still.

Hayley pulled the plug from the drain, and the sound of water seeping from the tub was wonderfully normal. Quickly she dried herself and pulled on the night-gown she'd laid out. Had it been premonition that had made her choose one that was both comforting and demure? Or had she chosen the old-fashioned rose-printed gown because she'd been feeling feminine after her lovemaking with Grant? She knew only that as the soft fabric unfolded over her body, she was glad she had selected something that covered her from neck to ankles.

Trembling with belated reaction, she knelt to pet Bluster, but just as she reached for him the dog dashed away, making a beeline for the open cabinet.

"You're getting bath oil all over your paws," Hayley lamented with a groan, not relishing the idea of having to bathe his feet. "I don't know how a nose as sensitive as yours can take being so close to that stuff."

The oil had to be cleaned up before she went to bed. The strong odor was already giving her a headache. She closed the bathroom door so that Bluster couldn't follow and trail bath oil through the rest of the house. In the kitchen she collected paper towels for mopping and liquid detergent to cut through the oil.

Bluster was inside the cupboard when she returned to the bathroom. He didn't seem interested in the oil but was whining softly and digging frantically at the back corner. "Look at the mess you're making!" she scolded.

He'd made chaos of the contents of the cupboard. He'd knocked over the four-pack of toilet paper, the aerosol can of tub-and-tile cleaner, the bottles of shampoo and hydrogen peroxide. Hayley removed the items one by one and wiped away any oil that had gotten on them, then reached inside for Bluster. "What's got you so riled up? Look, you've scratched the paint."

She spread paper towels over the spilled oil to soak up as much as possible. Bluster made a nuisance of himself as she worked, nudging her hands, trying to get back inside the cabinet. Finally she picked him up, held him over the sink while soaping and rinsing his feet, then dried his paws with a towel. "That ought to do it."

He didn't like being banished to the bedroom while she worked, and kept whining and lunging at the bathroom door. Hayley worked as fast as she could to get the oil cleaned up, then stuffed all the soiled paper towels into a plastic bag. Although she'd opened the small window above the tub, her head still ached from smelling the concentrated bath oil at such close range. Finally she sprinkled a light layer of talcum powder over the area to absorb any residual moisture and, hopefully, odor. All that remained was to clean the outside of the bottle and replace it next to the tub, although she suspected that it would be a long time before she used it again without feeling nauseous.

Bluster's whining and thumping at the door were making her headache worse. Disgusted, she opened the door and let him back in the bathroom. With his usual single-mindedness, he darted straight to the cabinet and began digging at the back corner again. "Oh, no," she said, squatting. "Out you come. I've got to get this stuff put away so I can get some slee— Oh, Bluster, now look what you've done!"

She put the dog behind her and examined the damage. "Now, how do I repair—?"

On closer inspection, it wasn't a hole, as she'd first thought, but a large crack along the seam where the two side panels met. She pushed tentatively on the damaged panel. Paint split, outlining a square. She pushed again, gently, and the entire square moved.

A secret panel! The thought raised goose bumps on her arms. She sat down on the floor, leaned against the wall and groaned.

Secret panels! Ghosts. Cryptic warnings. Her life was beginning to resemble a bad Gothic novel. Maybe Grant was right. Maybe living alone had been just too dull, her mind was creating some excitement.

No! She wasn't twisted enough to think up Arthur Ramsey. And she certainly wasn't imagining the square of wood Bluster had knocked loose. It probably wasn't anything as dramatic as a secret panel, anyway; it was probably just a door to some pipes or a patch over a mouse hole in the original wood.

While she was absorbed in thought, Bluster took advantage of her inattention and dashed back to scratch in the corner of the cabinet again. Hayley reached for him, but it was too late. The loose panel landed on the floor of the cabinet with a thunk. Instead of being deterred, Buster became even more excited and, barking and whining, clawed furiously at the exposed area.

"What has gotten into you?" Hayley muttered. Getting him out of the cabinet was a physical battle. "Is there an old mouse carcass or something in there?"

That prospect didn't cheer her. She just wanted to get the panel back in place and the stuff back in the cabinet and go to bed. But not before she took two aspirin for her throbbing head.

She banished Bluster to the bedroom again, and returned to the cabinet, determined to get the job finished. She picked up the square of wood and examined it, and the hole it fit, as she might study a puzzle. It appeared simple enough: a square piece of wood, a square hole. She poised the panel over the opening and slipped it into place, but couldn't get it quite flush with the wood around it. Chips of paint rained on her hand as she gave the center of the panel a tap with her fist.

Oh, great! Now lead poisoning, she thought. The O'Keefes had undoubtedly used latex, but there could be layers of old, lead-based paint beneath. She tapped the panel again. A movement inside the wall piqued her curiosity. She paused, waiting, half afraid it was something alive, but there was no other movement. Working gingerly, lest whatever had fallen inside the wall was something dead, she used her fingernails to pry the panel loose, then heaved a sigh of relief as it popped out and she saw what was behind it.

Unless someone had laid a pet to rest in a small box and wrapped it in a brown paper bag, it was no corpse. She took a fold of the paper between her thumb and forefinger and gave it a swift tug. The bundle slid easily from the opening. Hayley stared at it a moment before summoning enough courage to pick it up.

Handling the fragile, age-brittled paper with great care, Hayley opened the bag. The first thing she noticed was the familiar scent of gardenia. The object in the bag was permeated with it. With trembling fingers, Hayley peeled aside a yellow lace-edged handkerchief and found a book bound in fine leather. It was Cynthia Ramsey's Bible. The words *Holy Bible* and her name were written on the front in gold leaf, the pages were edged with gold, and a satin ribbon page marker was sewn into the binding.

As Hayley cradled the book in her hands, it fell open, and the source of the scent was revealed. Through the years, the gardenia blossom Cynthia had pressed between the pages had become part of them. Hayley traced that dark brown silhouette with her forefinger, imagining the white flower aging within the pages and bleeding its fragrant oil into the Scriptures.

The satin ribbon marked the Old Testament Book of Ruth. Someone had drawn a cross in the margin next to the sixteenth verse of the first chapter. Hayley sighed, "Oh, Cynthia," as she read the familiar passage:

" ...for whither thou goest, I will go; and where thou lodgest, I will lodge.... "

What other passage would a woman contemplating an elopement have marked?

Carefully she flipped through the pages, searching for other verses similarly marked. The ornate family-history pages in the center of the book bore the names of Cynthia's mother and father, their birthdates and the date of her mother's death. Hayley calculated that Cynthia had been only six years old when her mother had died. What must it have been like for her, growing up without a mother? And Arthur—what must it have been like for a man to raise a daughter alone in the late 1930s? Had that awesome burden made him overprotective and tyrannical?

She thought sadly of the tragic lives of father and daughter as she searched through the rest of the pages, careful not to shatter the brittle gardenia when she reached it. There were no more marked verses, but toward the last of the pages she found what appeared to be an invoice from Withers & Bertram Automotive Garage. Hayley didn't recognize the name of the garage, but the street address placed it in the downtown business district.

If it was a bill, Hayley reflected, there would be a date. But it wasn't a bill. It was a poem of love, written in a man's heavy script, and decorated with scrollwork and flowers and hearts. The artwork was not that of a man with artistic talent, Hayley thought, so much as that of a man with a romantic heart.

She recognized the poem from English 231: Byron, with his flowing cadences and sentimental theme.

> She walks in beauty, like the night
> Of cloudless climes and starry skies;
> And all that's best of dark and bright
> Meet in her aspect and her eyes:
> Thus mellowed to that tender lights
> Which heaven to gaudy day denies.

Hayley imagined Cynthia reading and rereading the poem, dreaming of her lover.

It struck her, then, the sequence of events during Cynthia's appearance: the urgent warning, the cabinet door opening, the bath oil rolling and spilling so it would have to be cleaned up. Cynthia had wanted her to find the Bible; she had as much as pointed a ghostly finger at it.

When she thought about the hidden Bible analytically instead of romantically, Hayley realized that it shouldn't have been there at all. Obviously Cynthia had hidden the Bible to keep her father from seeing it, but wouldn't a young woman sentimental enough to press flowers and hide love poems have taken the Bible with her when she eloped? A flower from her lover? It would have been the first thing she put in her suitcase.

If she'd had time to pack. Perhaps Cynthia hadn't known her lover was coming for her until he'd tapped on her window. Or perhaps she'd known he was coming, but not on which night or at what time.

Warn him. He's watching. Perhaps Arthur had somehow learned of their plans and was watching for her lover. If they'd had to leave in a hurry, she might have fled with no baggage at all.

Fear knotted in Hayley's chest. What if Arthur had been waiting and watching? What could he have done to the man who came to take away his daughter? Perhaps Cynthia had been afraid of just such an eventuality. Could it have been Cynthia's fear she'd sensed when Grant started to come into her room?

Bluster banged on the door, protesting his banishment. Hayley put the poem back in the Bible and closed it, then carefully put it, the handkerchief and the brown paper on the top shelf of the cabinet. She haphazardly replaced the wooden panel and shoved the toilet paper, tile cleaner and other objects into the cabinet before letting the little hellion in.

The dog went to the cabinet, gave it an exploratory sniff, grimaced comically when he got a noseful of talcum powder, and walked over to Hayley's feet and whimpered for attention. Hayley picked him up and hugged him. "Poor Bluster. This ghost business is hard on your nerves, too, isn't it?"

She knew without a doubt it was Arthur Ramsey's ghost that called her names, but for the first time Hayley wondered why she had so easily accepted that the woman who'd appeared in the bathroom was the ghost of Cynthia Ramsey, where there was no reason in the world to believe that Cynthia Ramsey was even dead. She put it on the list of questions she'd ask if she ever found anyone who'd known her.

She carried Bluster to the kitchen, where she checked the phone book for a listing for Withers & Bertram Auto Garage.

There was none. There were, however, four residential listings under the name Withers, and three under the name Bertram.

Although she was exhausted, she scarcely slept all night. There were moments when, after flopping around in a futile attempt to get comfortable, she was tempted to go over to the bait shop and rouse Grant and say, "Hold me." But that would have necessitated explanations for why she couldn't sleep, and she wasn't about to tell Grant about Cynthia's visit when he didn't believe her about Arthur.

Would she believe him if the tables were turned? She honestly didn't know. Up to the moment when Arthur had shown up scowling at her, she would have sworn that ghosts existed only in folklore, horror novels and scary movies. That didn't stop her from feeling frustrated that Grant wouldn't trust her judgment. She didn't doubt for one instant that he cared about her, but was it enough that he cared, if he couldn't at least try to believe in her?

She replayed the visit from Cynthia in her mind and puzzled over the meaning of Cynthia's cryptic warnings. Behind closed eyes, she kept seeing Cynthia's Bible with the gardenia crushed in it and the romantic poem written on a garage invoice and decorated with childlike artwork.

Questions. Riddles. When the alarm clock went off, she rolled over to slap it into silence and muttered, "You've got to be kidding!" Then she grinned, realizing it was one of Grant's pet phrases.

She put on the suit closest to the closet door and fluffed her hair. Makeup would have to wait until she was stopped at traffic lights.

She waved to Grant as Bluster made his morning dash to the bait shop. Instead of just waving back, however, Grant jogged across the yard and reached Hayley just as she was getting into her car.

"No good-morning kiss?" he asked.

Smiling was an effort, but Hayley managed it as memories of their lovemaking rushed through her mind. "I might be persuaded."

After kissing her, he cupped her chin in his hand and studied her face. "You look tired."

"Restless night."

"For Arthur Ramsey?"

"No. Old Arthur didn't show up. I just . . . couldn't sleep."

"You should have stayed with me. We'd both have gotten a good night's sleep."

She pouted coquettishly. "Think so?"

His grin broadened as he pulled her close. "At least if we weren't able to sleep, we'd have had some pleasant alternatives."

"I didn't know you played chess."

"I don't."

"Monopoly? Trivial Pursuit?"

He shook his head. "I play a different game."

"Oh?" She looked up at him tauntingly.

"I'll teach you," he said, holding her so tightly against him that she could scarcely breathe. "Lesson one. And here's lesson two." He kissed her until her knees felt weak.

"If there's a lesson three," Hayley rasped, "maybe we'd better wait until I get home from work."

"It's a date."

TIRED, AND ANXIOUS TO GET HOME, Hayley left work earlier than usual. When she pulled into her driveway, she immediately noticed that the dog run was up. Next to it, Slim and Grant were working like industrious beavers, hammering and sawing, so intent on their task that they only nodded hello. Bluster and his father were stretched out on the grass in identical poses, supervising the construction.

"What are you building?"

"A doghouse," Slim replied. "Dog's got to have shade and shelter."

"Of course." Hayley entered the dog run and walked its circumference, then complimented Slim on a job well done.

"Grant helped."

At the mention of his name, Grant stopped his sawing and looked at her. Hayley tipped her head in a salute. "Then I guess I owe you a thank-you, too."

He wanted to kiss her. It was clear in the way he looked at her. Hayley was unable to control the answering flush that rose in her cheeks as their eyes met.

"Just being neighborly," Grant said. His expression told her that he had read her response.

Hayley was certain Slim had been aware of every nuance of the silent exchange, but no one would ever have known it as he picked up a board and aligned it with the one he'd just nailed in place. He drove in an anchoring nail, then abruptly put his hammer aside and probed his shirt pocket for a folded piece of paper.

"Before I forget... I asked at the hardware store about anyone who might have known Cynthia Ramsey or the man she married. This man was his business partner. They owned a garage together for a while down on Central. He's retired now. Mr. Walters down at the hardware store looked up his number for you."

Hayley caught the censure in Grant's expression as she accepted the slip of paper and thanked Slim. "If you men would excuse me a moment, I think I'll go give this Mister—"

Her heart lodged in her throat as she glanced at the paper. "Withers a call. Can I get either of you something to drink while I'm inside? Water? Tea? Beer?"

Slim picked up his hammer and positioned a nail. "Nothing for me, thanks."

"I could use a glass of water."

"I'll bring it out," Hayley said, but Grant had already laid aside his saw.

"No need for you to make a special trip. I'll go in with you."

Hayley didn't have the energy to argue with him, so she led the way into the house. As soon as they were inside, Grant said, "Please don't call that man."

Hayley tossed her purse on the sofa but held on to the paper Slim had given her. "It's none of your business."

"*You* are my business."

"Because we made love once?"

"Twice!" he corrected, then added sarcastically, "How quickly you forget."

"I haven't forgotten anything." *Not a single, delicious detail.*

He put his hands on her shoulders and looked down at her. "I can almost believe that from the look in your eyes."

She sighed and relaxed into his arms. "I don't want to fight with you, Grant."

"Then let it go, Hayley."

"I can't. I have to find out—"

"You're becoming obsessed."

She jerked away from him. "I am *not* obsessed."

"The first time I met you, you were talking about Cynthia Ramsey eloping in a rowboat."

"Everyone around here knows how Lovers' Lake got its name. Natural curiosity doesn't add up to an obsession."

"You were fascinated by the romance of it. So fascinated that you invented—"

Hayley felt as though she'd been doused by a bucket of cold water. "Say it! I was so fascinated that I invented Arthur Ramsey's ghost."

God, what would he think if she told him about Cynthia's visit?

Grant sighed in frustration, and tried to put his arms around her. He was relieved when, instead of pulling away, she slipped her arms around his waist and rested her cheek on his chest. Encouraged, he said gently, "Let's go somewhere—out to dinner, take in a movie, get away from this house, forget all about Arthur Ramsey and his daughter."

"You don't understand. I can't just run away from this. I've got to deal with it."

"You've got to let go of it."

"I have a telephone call to make." She squirmed out of his embrace, stalked to the kitchen and set the paper beside the phone. Her hands trembled as she picked up the receiver and punched in the number.

Grant followed her, and their eyes met as the phone on the other end of the line began ringing. She tilted her chin defiantly, and asked to speak to Mr. Withers, then introduced herself. Mr. Withers was willing to talk to her so she agreed to go to the Withers home, and wrote down directions on the notepad next to the phone. Grant was scowling when she replaced the receiver. "We had a date tonight."

"I'll be home in an hour or two."

"Don't hurry on my account. I may decide to take in a movie or two."

After an awkward silence, Hayley walked to the cabinet and took out a glass. "I believe you wanted some water."

9

GRANT INTERCEPTED HER as she moved toward the refrigerator and with his arms stretched out on either side of her, pinned her against the countertop. He pressed closer. Looking down at her arms wedged between them, he wrenched the glass out of her hand and set it on the counter with a thunk, then wrapped his arms around her. "The only thing I want is you."

He claimed her mouth in a rough kiss, a kiss of dominance. Startled, Hayley stiffened in resistance, but gradually as the kiss became softer and less demanding, she relaxed, her lips parted under his and she slid her arms over his shoulders.

Grant was out of breath when he finally lifted his face from hers. "We'll go out for dinner when you get back."

It was more a question than a demand, and charmed by the subtle repentance in the gesture, Hayley kissed his cheek. "Slim's going to be wondering where you are."

"Slim knows where I am, and I'd be very surprised if he didn't suspect exactly what I've been doing while I'm in here."

"He doesn't miss much," Hayley agreed, and wondered what Slim would think about the ghosts.

SHE FOUND THE WITHERS house easily. It was built in the rambling ranch style popular in the fifties, surrounded by a lush, rolling lawn and semitropical foliage. Thomas and Gladys Withers met her at the door and welcomed her with an easy hospitality that matched their Southern accents.

"So you bought the old Ramsey place," Thomas Withers said, as they settled into chairs in the den. "I noticed someone had fixed it up the last time I was out that way."

"Most of the credit goes to the couple who sold it to me," Hayley replied. "But I fell in love with it at first sight. When I heard the legend about Cynthia Ramsey eloping by rowboat, I became curious about her. I understand her father was something of a recluse."

"Recluse?" Withers echoed, with a snort of derision. "The man was a gallon short of a tankload, if you ask me."

"Insane?" Hayley asked.

"No, not insane. Just mean as a rattlesnake, especially when it came to his daughter. Cynthia didn't say much about him, not wanting to be disrespectful, but you could tell she was cowed by him. He wouldn't let her go anywhere but to church, and even there, he didn't like her socializing much."

"She thought he was . . . peculiar . . . because he was lonely," Mrs. Withers said. "Apparently he never got over her mother's death."

"I understood you knew the man Cynthia eloped with."

"I did more than know him," Thomas told her. "Martin was the best friend I had in the world. We were in business together, but he was more like a brother to me."

"Was he from this area, too?"

"Naw. Martin was from Illinois. That was one of the things Old Man Ramsey had against him."

"Because he was from Illinois?"

Withers chuckled. "I can tell from your accent that you're not from around here. Hasn't anyone called you a Yankee yet?"

"I'm afraid so," Hayley admitted. "More than once. People warned me that Southerners were still prejudiced against Northerners, but I didn't believe it until I got here."

"It was worse forty years ago, believe me, especially here in the rural South."

"How did you and Martin meet?"

"The army. We were in the same unit in World War II. Motor pool. Martin had worked on tractors all his life, and I'd always tinkered with engines. By the time the war ended, there wasn't a motor in existence that we couldn't keep purring."

"So you decided to go into the car repair business."

"Not right away. We'd joked about it during the war, but you know how it is. As soon as the word came down that the war was over, everybody scattered in different directions and all those big plans we made seemed kind of silly."

He scratched his chin thoughtfully. "No, it was almost a year after we hit Stateside before Martin got in touch with me. He just kind of showed up one day, and we got to reminiscing and talking about our old plans and—well, nothing had gone right for him since he got home, and I wasn't exactly setting the world on fire working as a soda jerk. So we decided we didn't have anything to lose. We both had a little pay saved up, so we rented a building and hung out a sign and worked our backsides off."

A returning soldier. Up until that moment, Hayley hadn't figured Grant to be a piece of the puzzle, other than the emotions he stirred in her. Now she saw the parallel emerging between Grant and Cynthia's lover. "What exactly—I hope you don't think I'm being nosy, but I'd really like to know—what did you mean when you said nothing had gone right for Martin after the war?"

"Nothing was the same for him after he got back to Illinois. His girl had married someone else. She'd gone to Chicago to live with relatives and work in a defense plant. She was going to save up some money for when Martin came home. But she was young, and Martin was a long way away, and there were plenty of sailors from out at the Great Lakes. Anyway, she married one of them."

"He must have been heartbroken."

Thomas shrugged. "Disillusioned is probably a better word. They'd just been kids when they were courting, and he hadn't seen her in three years."

Disillusioned, Hayley thought, and mused aloud, "He couldn't go home again."

"That's about the size of it," Thomas said. "His folks were pretty sickly, too. His dad had been in declining health for years, and the farm was in bad shape. He died a month after Martin got home, and Martin's mother went a few months later. It happens that way sometimes, with old folks. And Martin—well, he had never cared for farming. He had an uncle a few years older than him who jumped at the chance to take over the farm. He was newly wed, with a kid on the way. So one day Martin signed it over to him and took the next train to Florida."

"How did he meet Cynthia?"

"At church. How else? I was courting Gladys, here, and she sang in the choir with Cynthia. One Sunday a month they had a covered dish dinner after the services, and I talked Martin into tagging along with me one Sunday. One look at Cynthia was all it took."

"That's all it took for Cynthia, too," Mrs. Withers said. "She was a very quiet girl. With the war and all, she hadn't had a chance to meet many boys, and even when she did, her father usually ran them off in a hurry. But Martin was different. He was a man, not a boy, and he refused to back off. And Cynthia was head over heels. It was the first time she had cared enough about a man to stand up to her father. That just made him that much more determined to break them up."

"I'd like to show you something," Hayley said. She had brought the poem written on the invoice. She took it from her purse and laid it on the coffee table in front of Thomas Withers.

Withers picked it up and stared at it for a long time. Visibly moved, he held it out for his wife's perusal. "Look at this, Gladys. Why, I haven't seen that letterhead since we reprinted without Martin's name."

"Then that's his handwriting?"

"Oh, undeniably," Mrs. Withers said. "This is the note Martin sent Cynthia when he was planning their elopement." She looked at Hayley. "Where did you get this?"

"I found Cynthia's Bible stashed in a niche in the wall in my bathroom. The poem was in it. Along with a pressed gardenia."

Gladys Withers smiled. "He used to pick gardenias for Cynthia. They were her favorite flowers."

"You say he sent this note to her when they were planning their elopement?"

"Yes. Her father had forbidden her to see him, even in the churchyard after church. So he gave me this note for her, and he said to tell her it had a secret message, and that she was supposed to read his hearts."

"Hearts? Plural?"

"Yes. I thought that was odd, too, but he made me practice saying it."

"The Bible was one of the reasons I called you," Hayley told them. "I'm sure Cynthia would like to have it. I thought perhaps if you had her current address, I could send it to her."

Mr. and Mrs. Withers exchanged odd looks. Then Mrs. Withers said, cautiously, "I know Cynthia would want it, but I'm afraid I can't help you. You see—" She glanced at her husband, as if asking whether she should go on. He nodded. "We never heard from Cynthia and Martin after they left. We always thought that was a little odd."

"Not at first," Withers added. "Martin didn't tell me what he had planned, because he didn't want to put me on the spot if Old Man Ramsey came around asking questions. If Ramsey managed to find him, he wanted it to be after they'd been married long enough to make an annulment impractical—if you know what I mean."

Hayley grinned. "I understand."

Withers continued. "He'd scraped together as much cash as he could. He signed over his half of the business to me, and I gave him the cash we had on hand, but it wasn't nearly what his half was worth. He was supposed to let me know where to send the rest after they got settled. Only we never heard from them."

"I think that was probably Cynthia's doing," Gladys said. "She was probably so relieved to get away from her father that she didn't want to risk his finding her."

"You've got to realize that things were different back then. It wasn't unusual for people to fall out of touch, even families. But Martin... I sure thought I'd hear from him."

Hayley took a deep breath. It was time to ask a difficult question. "Was there any indication that Arthur Ramsey was *violent* with her?"

Gladys paused, considering her reply. "I wouldn't rule it out. By today's standards, anyway. Back then, kids got their hides tanned with razor straps and belts, and no one thought a thing about it. Arthur Ramsey was a tyrant. It took a lot of guts for Cynthia to stand up to him."

"Martin was scared for her, I can tell you that," Thomas said. "Cynthia didn't come right out and tell him she thought her father might hurt her physically, but she was afraid. Martin wanted her out of there, no matter what it took."

They fell into a thoughtful silence. Hayley had learned more than she'd dared hope about Martin Bertram, some of it disturbing. But there was one more question to be asked—a question whose answer just might destroy her peace of mind. And it was only by recalling the translucent figure of Cynthia Ramsey and her desperate pleas that she was able to bring herself to voice it.

"Have you ever considered... Was there ever any question that Martin and Cynthia didn't leave the house together that night, and safely?"

"Not at the time. Just as Martin suspected, Ramsey raised a ruckus with the sheriff, demanding that his daughter be found and that Martin be arrested. He wanted to call in the FBI. There was a massive investigation. Cynthia was over twenty-one, but Arthur insisted she wouldn't have left of her own free will. I think the sheriff wanted to find them so he could get it straight from Cynthia that she hadn't been kidnapped, and the whole thing would be off his shoulders. But nobody ever found hide nor hair of them, and I remember thinking that Martin was a genius."

"You said, 'Not at the time,'" Hayley reminded.

Withers frowned. "Later, when we didn't hear from them, I have to admit it crossed my mind that the whole thing was mighty peculiar. As though they'd both vanished from the face of the earth." Deep in reflection, he shook his head slowly. "I can't deny that I'd feel a whole lot better about the whole thing if we'd heard *something* from Martin."

"Thomas has been waiting for a postcard or a Christmas card for over forty-five years," Gladys Withers said. "I wish Martin had sent one."

They chatted for a few minutes more, then Hayley thanked Mr. and Mrs. Withers for talking to her and left. The interview had confirmed theories and reinforced doubts she would rather have had debunked. Most disturbing of all were the parallels revealed between Grant and Martin Bertram. She'd assumed that Arthur Ramsey had tuned in to her feelings because of the similarities between Cynthia and herself. Now she realized that Grant was as much a part of Arthur's restless hauntings as she; his presence was as much a catalyst as hers.

She knew with absolute certainty that Grant could be in danger. She had to make him see it and accept it. How, she didn't know. How was she supposed to make him believe that a ghost he didn't believe in could possibly pose a threat to him? Or that a woman no one could be sure was dead had come into her bathroom to warn him?

He was standing on the pier staring out at the water when she got home, a melancholy figure with his hands in his back pockets. Bluster, who'd been sitting at Grant's feet, heard Hayley approaching, leaped up and, barking, ran toward her. As if awakened from a trance, Grant pulled his hands from his pockets and looked in her direction before coming to greet her.

They didn't speak immediately, but he stretched his arm across her shoulders in a gentle caress.

With Hayley tucked under his arm, her body voluptuous and warm next to his, Grant felt at peace for the first time since he'd watched her take that slip of paper from Slim. He was curious what, if anything, she'd learned, but he didn't want to ask. He'd hear about it soon enough. She'd be full of new information and theories, and would start talking about ghosts, and they'd be at odds again.

God, how he dreaded the thought of it. She'd been in his bed two and a half hours, and he had become so accustomed to her presence that the bed felt strange and empty without her. After walking her home, he'd spent the rest of the night tossing and turning, worrying about her. Oddly enough, it had felt good to worry about her; he felt better about himself than he had in a long, long time—probably because it had been so long since he'd cared enough to worry about another human being.

The night was tranquil, the chorus of crickets soothing to the nerves. There was no breeze, and the moon on the surface of the dark, still water was a perfect reflection of the brilliant disk that hung high in the cloudless sky.

"It's so peaceful," Hayley said, letting her body lean solidly against his. "Everyone talks about Florida's sunshine, but I like the nights better."

Savoring the serenity of the moment, Grant smiled in the darkness, then quoted, "'Thus mellowed to that tender light/ Which heaven to gaudy day denies.'"

The effect on Hayley was electric, but not what he'd expected. She tensed from head to toe, all the softness in her turning to unyielding stone.

"Hayley?"

She trembled. "Do you always quote Byron?"

"Is that what that was?"

Her voice tremulous, she repeated the question.

"No. I don't always quote anybody, *especially* Byron. I don't even know where I learned that. Probably had to memorize it in freshman English. I guess the night, and having you next to me, put me in a poetic mood."

She was still tense, still trembling.

"Do you have a thing about Byron?" he asked.

"I... It's just... *odd* that you would quote that particular piece of poetry tonight."

"It just popped into my mind, and it seemed... appropriate."

"Popped into your mind," she murmured. She looked him full in the face. "I have something to show you."

He tilted his head toward the bait shop. "Let's go inside."

"Not here. Let's go out somewhere for dinner. I'll show you over dessert."

They chose a quiet out-of-the-way restaurant. Neither of them finished their meal and neither wanted dessert. After the waiter served them coffee that would sit ignored in the cups, Hayley took out the poem and slid it across the table so Grant could read it.

"This is the poem I quoted tonight," he said.

Hayley nodded gravely.

"Where did you get this?"

"I found it in Cynthia Ramsey's Bible. That's the note that Martin Bertram sent to her before they eloped."

"Where would you get Cynthia Ramsey's Bible? And how could you know that—"

"Do you see the letterhead there? Withers & Bertram. Bertram was the man Cynthia was in love with. The man I talked to today was Martin Bertram's partner. His wife delivered this note to Cynthia at church one Sunday while they were both sitting in the choir loft. There's some kind of secret code in it."

Grant muttered a blistering expletive. "Ghosts weren't enough. Now we're into secret codes?"

Hayley looked as though he'd struck her. Her eyes filled with tears, and she choked back a sob. "I don't have anyone else to tell. And even if I did, I would have to tell you. You're a part of this, too."

"A part of what?"

"I guess you think it's just some weird coincidence that you suddenly started spouting that poem tonight."

"I told you, I was feeling poetic."

"You didn't even know what it was you were quoting."

"Come on," he said, counting out bills for the check the waiter had left on the table. "Let's get out of here."

"Where are we going?" she asked, when he turned onto the main highway, in the opposite direction from home.

"Neutral territory," he said. "A place where we can be alone. And comfortable."

On the edge of town they came to a string of hotels. He pulled into the registration area of a well-known chain and parked. "I'll get us checked in."

It was a typical hotel room, with a small desk, remote-control television and two queen-size beds. Hayley stood just inside the door and stared at the floral still life bolted to the wall. "Are you all right?" Grant asked.

"I've never been to a hotel with a man before."

She seemed small and lost. Vulnerable. He touched her shoulder reassuringly. "I didn't bring you here to insult you."

She swallowed, then said softly, "We can't leave Bluster in the dog run all night. What if he digs himself out?"

Grant frowned. "I forgot all about him. Look, why don't you get comfortable. Take a bath. Relax. I'll get Bluster and grab another T-shirt for you."

Hayley wanted to protest, but it made sense for them to have a neutral place to talk. Grant sensed her turmoil and kissed her cheek. "It'll be fine."

He was gone almost an hour, which gave her time for a leisurely bath. Stretched out in the tub, she had to admit to herself that it was a relief being away from her house, nice not to have to worry about whether Cynthia Ramsey was going to come spinning into the bathroom, or if Arthur was going to show up and call her ugly names.

She spread the body lotion provided by the hotel over her arms and legs, then wrapped herself in a towel and sprinted to the bed. There was something decadent about being between hotel sheets without a stitch of clothing on, and she savored the illicit thrill. Lying back against the pillows wedged against the headboard, she could easily have gone to sleep. Instead, she took the poem from her purse and studied it.

"Read his hearts." His hearts! The tiny hearts in Martin Bertram's crude artwork! The ribbons, flowers and scrollwork encircled the text and wove between the lines, but hearts appeared only under certain letters within the text.

Hayley grabbed the pen and notepad next to the phone on the nightstand and began writing down the letters.

She walks in beauty, like the night
Of cloudless climes and starry skies;
And all that's best of dark and bright
Meet in her aspect and her eyes.
Thus mellowed to that tender lights
Which heaven to gaudy day denies.

She'd just finished writing when Grant returned, with Bluster under one arm and a bag under the other. "Are you sure this is legal?" she asked, when he put the pup on the bed beside her.

"We'll be all right as long as he's quiet." He sat on the edge of the bed and watched her pet the dog.

"You're the sexiest woman I've ever been in a hotel room with."

"I'm afraid to ask how many women I just beat out."

"If there'd been thousands, you'd still win," he said. "But for the record, there haven't been nearly as many as you seem to think."

His admiration made her feel sexy. Seductive. Desirable. She leaned forward, slipped her arms around his neck and kissed him. His hands caressed her bare back. She ended the kiss with a languid sigh and rested her cheek against his.

"We've got to talk," she said.

"I know," he agreed, not bothering to hide his regret. He pulled a T-shirt out of the bag he'd brought. "I'm not anxious to cover up those shoulders, but if you'd be more comfortable, I might be less distracted— What are you grinning at?"

"You." She put on the shirt. "When I first met you, I thought you were a grouch and a half. I didn't expect you to be sweet."

"Don't spread it around, huh? A rumor like that could destroy my reputation."

"My silence will cost you," she returned suggestively.

"I look forward to your making me pay." His teasing smile faded when he caught sight of the poem on her lap. "You've been reading that again?"

"Better," she said. "I'm not only sexy, I'm smart. I broke the code."

"I'm going to sit down for this." He took the pillows from the unoccupied bed and propped them against the headboard beside Hayley. After kicking off his shoes, he swung his legs onto the bed and arranged the pillows until he was comfortable. Then he turned to Hayley and said, "So, Sherlock, what'd you figure out?"

"It was really simple," she replied. "I just looked for the hearts, see? And look what it spelled out." She handed him the notepad, where she'd written the marked letters.

Grant read aloud. "Three o'clock in the morning. Thursday."

"It's the time and the day," Hayley said. "It's how he let Cynthia know when he was coming."

"That's interesting."

"You're not the least bit interested," she accused.

"Hayley, I know it's exciting for you to have this, to figure this out, because you're so hung up on Cynthia

Ramsey. But look at it for what it is. It's just a note a man sent a woman a long time ago. It doesn't *prove* anything. No one's ever said they didn't elope. Frame it. Hang it on the wall as a tribute to the woman who used to live in your house. But don't—"

He reached for her, drew her into his arms, and hugged her tightly. "Please, Hayley, let go of this obsession so we can go on with our lives."

She gratefully accepted the comfort of his strength and warmth. Gathering the sleeve of his shirt in her hand, she clung to it as she spoke. "I'd give anything to be able to let it go, Grant. But I didn't make it up. Won't you please listen to me?"

"I have listened."

"No, Grant. I mean really listen, without interrupting, or giving me that long-suffering, patronizing look, or closing your mind."

"You make me sound like such a jerk."

His sadness went straight to Hayley's heart. She closed her eyes as he reached over and brushed his thumb across her cheek.

"I'm so scared for you," she said.

"For me? You're the one in trouble. I'm terrified for you, and what this is doing to you."

"You're a part of it, too. Oh, Grant, *please* listen."

Grant shifted his shoulders. "That's the second time you've accused me of not listening. I'm all ears now, lady. Talk."

She raised her head. "You won't interrupt?"

"I'd sooner cut out my tongue."

She started talking. The words flowed out of her, detail after detail. About the sensation of menace that had made her desperate to get him away from her room. About Cynthia's visit and her pleas to warn "him" that "he" was watching. About the bath oil spilling, and Bluster digging at the wall and finding the Bible. About Martin Bertram's desperation to get Cynthia out of the house because they were afraid of her father. About Thomas Withers's never having heard from his best friend and partner.

She told him what she'd learned about Martin Bertram, and how he'd been a disillusioned veteran. "Don't you see? I thought it was just me—that because I was about Cynthia Ramsey's age and had started having romantic feelings, Arthur was responding to them. To me. But it's you, too. Martin Bertram came home from World War II and nothing was the same. He felt he couldn't go home again, so he started a new life, and he met Cynthia. You felt the same way when you came home from Desert Storm, and you bought the bait shop and you met *me.* After I got over the shock of having Arthur Ramsey around, I never felt threatened by him. *You* were the catalyst for the impending danger I felt in my room, not me. And Cynthia didn't come back to warn me about her father. She wanted me to warn *you.*"

Grant had listened as long as he could. "Against what?"

"Not what, who. Cynthia said, 'He's watching.' Grant, I think her father knew about Martin Bertram and was waiting for him. And now he knows about you, and he's waiting for you."

"Waiting for what?"

"Something awful!" She hugged him, clinging. "If we knew what really happened the night Martin came for Cynthia, then we'd know what to be afraid of."

"They eloped that night, Hayley. He rowed the boat up to the yard, and they left together, and Old Man Ramsey went insane because of it."

"There's no proof of that. Martin's partner knew about his plans, and Martin rented a boat. The owner saw him leave for my house. But there was a massive manhunt for them, and the sheriff couldn't find a single person who'd seen them in the boat or on shore together. The boat was found adrift. Everyone assumed that Martin had rowed ashore in an isolated clearing, then pushed the boat back into the water, knowing it would be found and returned to the owner—and that no one would know where they'd gone ashore."

"Which is probably exactly what he did," Grant said. "It makes perfect sense. In fact, it's quite ingenious."

Hayley pulled away from him. "For a man who refuses to believe in ghosts because he can't see them, you're certainly willing to believe in a story that has never been proved."

"But there's no reason to believe it didn't happen exactly the way everyone thinks, either." The expression in his eyes seemed to be daring her to come up with some reason for doubt.

"Oh, yes, there is! Cynthia's Bible!" she said triumphantly. "With the flower he'd picked for her and the poem he'd written to her! It would have been the first thing she packed—or the only thing she took with her."

Grant gave a resigned sigh. "That's the most convincing argument you've ever come up with."

"Then you believe me?"

"I believe," he said, caressing her cheek with his fingertips, "that no matter what happened or is still happening in your house, we have to get to the bottom of it before the two of us can concentrate on our relationship."

"So what do we do?"

Grant looked at her a long time before answering. "We put the ghosts to rest, of course."

10

"HOW?" HAYLEY ASKED.

"I was hoping you might have some ideas."

After a thoughtful pause, Hayley said, "It would help if we could find out what really happened that night."

"That's kind of tricky, considering that the only three people who knew for sure were Arthur, Cynthia and Martin Bertram."

"Maybe we should ask them."

An uncomfortable silence followed. Then Hayley sat up ramrod straight and stared levelly into Grant's eyes and repeated, "Maybe we *should* ask them."

"I agree."

Her eyes widened. "What did you say?"

"I said, I agree."

Hayley could hardly believe it. "You really think so?"

"I told you before that I wanted to call Arthur's bluff."

"You were being facetious. That was when you didn't believe Arthur existed."

"I'm still not convinced he does."

"Then what—?"

"Whether or not he exists for me, he exists for you."

So he still doesn't believe me, Hayley thought in frustration. "I don't like what you're insinuating."

With his finger under her chin, he tilted her face up and forced her to look at him. "It's time we confronted this situation head-on. If he shows up, and we both see him, then we'll know for sure."

She turned her head and twisted away from him. "And if I see him and you don't?"

"Then we'll know something else. Either way, we'll know *something*. We can move forward."

His position had softened. She would be unfair not to acknowledge his effort at compromise. "I want to do it as soon as possible," she said.

"Tomorrow night?"

She nodded.

"Good idea," he agreed, putting his arm around her. It didn't take much persuasion to get her to snuggle up to him. Together, they eased back onto the pillows.

"I'm so tired," she murmured.

He kissed her temple. "Take tomorrow off."

"From work?"

He chuckled. "Yes, from work." He kissed her briefly. "Call in sick."

"I don't know—"

"You could use the rest."

"Maybe, but—"

"You know I'm right." He kissed her again. "The company's not going to fold if you skip one day. We don't have to check out until noon." Nudging her hair aside with his cheek, he blew in her ear and whispered, "You can call them from bed."

"Will you dial for me?"

Suddenly his hands were all over her, soothing, stimulating. His lips were just as busy on her neck. "I'll pretend to be your doctor if you want me to."

"That...won't be...necessary. I get...three days...personal leave...a...ahhh...year."

"Do you know what it does to me...to know...that you don't have on...anything...but my shirt?"

"Let me check." She spread her fingers over the front of his jeans. "Oh, my. Hot...hard—"

"The better to love you with, my dear," he said, rolling over and straddling her. His body pressed heavily into hers and the bedding separating them only heightened their awareness of each other. Grant kissed her on the mouth. On the face. On the neck. Just under her ear. And then he whispered, "I'm going to love you with it until we both collapse from sheer exhaustion, and after we've slept awhile, all naked and pressed together, I'm going to love you with it again."

She kneaded his back through his shirt, and twisted her head to whisper in his ear, "What are you waiting for, Mackenzie? Take off your clothes and get under the covers."

True to his promise, he loved her tenderly, as though he revered her; desperately, as though he couldn't get enough of her; slowly, as though they had a lifetime to while away in sensual pleasure; urgently, as though fate might wrench her from his arms at any moment. There were no sensitive areas he did not find and caress, no areas he caressed that did not melt under his touch like heated honeycomb.

Instinctively, Hayley loved him back—as tenderly, as desperately, as slowly, as urgently. Hungry for the feel of him, her hands explored, grasped and stroked. She found his secret, sensitive places and reveled in her power to arouse him.

She'd never loved or been loved with such ferocity or abandon. Replete, she slept in his arms as soundly as a child exhausted from play, and awoke to the sweetness of his kiss and the thrill of his touch to love and be loved again.

At eight she called her office. At nine-thirty, they ordered fresh fruits, croissants and champagne from room service. At noon, they got out of bed and showered together, letting the hot water and steam soothe their love-worn bodies. At one, she tucked the tail of the shirt Grant had brought her into the waistband of the skirt she had worn to work the day before. With Bluster excitedly sniffing the air, they drove to a fast-food restaurant, then took their lunch to a park and picnicked in the deserted gazebo while Bluster discovered the joys of acorns and pinecones.

There were long stretches of silence as they sat in the dappled sunlight, but they were neither awkward nor embarrassing. To Hayley, they seemed to be filled with unspoken words of fulfillment and the echoes of endearments whispered during their lovemaking. The silence cloaked her like the warmth of a down comforter on a winter night. She didn't want to talk of their love or of ghosts, or of the past or the future. She just wanted to bask in that soothing silence punctuated only by birdsong and breeze-ruffled trees. She knew the silence couldn't last forever, yet she felt a twinge of sadness when Grant spoke.

"Hayley."

She turned to him and saw love in the depths of his eyes.

"Last night," he said, "was—"

Hayley smiled. "For me, too. I'll never forget it."

He felt compelled to touch her and put his hand on her shoulders. "It was special, Hayley. *Everything* with you is."

She reached up to touch his hand with her own and pressed his palm against her skin, awakening a thousand tactile memories of their lovemaking. She closed her eyes. "Do you think—is it possible—that it's so good between us because we're reenacting Cynthia and Martin's love?"

"That we're possessed by them?"

"Just...sensitive to their feelings, picking up on them, like—"

"Radio receivers?"

"You quoted Martin's poem."

"It wasn't Martin's poem, Hayley. It was Byron's. Sooner or later everyone reads Byron in school. It's a mood poem. 'Thus mellowed to that tender light' seemed appropriate to the moment."

"You picked a gardenia and put it in my hair."

"*Hayley!* Adam probably put flowers in Eve's hair in the Garden of Eden."

She laughed wryly. "Look where it got them."

"The same place it got us. Because the *feelings* were the same."

"So you think the poem and the gardenia were just coincidence?"

"Hayley, if two bees sting two people at opposite ends of the country, it's not 'just coincidence' that they both say, 'Damn!' and swat at them. A bee stung us, that's all. Just like it stung Cynthia and Martin."

"That's not a very romantic analogy."

"I'm not a very romantic guy."

She rubbed her cheek against the top of his hand. "Like Napoleon wasn't ambitious."

"You bring out the romance in my soul."

He rubbed his thumb over her cheek caressingly. Hayley closed her eyes.

"I wasn't expecting you. This," he said. "I didn't know what I was searching for, but falling in love was the last thing in the world I expected."

"They say it always happens when you least expect it." She opened her eyes and met his gaze and smiled. "Do you think it'll last?"

"Do you think it could ever end?" he asked, and kissed her before she could answer.

GRANT SQUEEZED HAYLEY'S hand, reluctant to let go of her. "I don't like you going in alone."

"I won't be alone. Bluster will be with me."

Grant cast a skeptical look at the pup tucked under her arm. "I am *not* reassured."

"He's like an alarm. He senses Arthur's presence before I do."

Before—or when you tense up? Grant wondered. He was trying to keep an open mind, he really was. And something strange was definitely going on in Hayley's house. But the idea of ghosts was still difficult for him to swallow. And he didn't like knowing that whatever was going on, Hayley was right smack-dab in the middle of it.

Mentally, emotionally, and perhaps even physically, she was vulnerable—that was the only reason he'd agreed to get involved in the madness. Without him, she was totally alone.

And without her, he'd be totally alone. She'd become so much a part of his life that he could no longer imagine life without her.

She stood on tiptoe and kissed his cheek. "Don't worry. Arthur doesn't come on duty until sunset. It's a ghosts' union or something."

It took every once of discipline he possessed to let her walk into her house—alone, except for a ridiculous little puppy.

Hayley stopped in the entryway and looked around her. Despite the familiarity of the furnishings, she felt detached standing among them, as though she'd been away a long, long time instead of less than a day; like someone who used to live there and had come back for a sentimental visit.

Shaking off the sense of déjà vu, she put Bluster down, then laughed as, predictably, he dashed for the kitchen. He was noisily scrounging in the bottom of his dish by the time she reached the pantry to take out fresh dog food for him.

She kept Grant's shirt on, but traded her skirt for a pair of jeans. She put away the groceries they'd bought, sliced cheese, washed fruit, put a tablecloth on the table and centered the candles on it. Then, restless, she picked up a magazine and thumbed through it. But between memories of the night before and anticipation of the night ahead, she couldn't concentrate, even on the fashion layouts. Eventually she put the magazine aside, hugged her knees and sighed. Grant had been wise to take her away for the night. It had been good to get away, good to have a change of scenery, good to be able to talk and make plans while out from under the shadow of Lovers' Lake and Cynthia and Martin's legendary elopement.

She looked down at Bluster, curled into a ball next to her on the couch. Her little ghost detector. He'd been quiet all afternoon, and now was sleeping peacefully. *Sleep now, little one*, she thought. *I have a feeling it's going to be a wild and woolly night.*

As planned, Grant knocked promptly at seven. His eyes were full of questions as their gazes met. Hayley shook her head—there'd been no sign of Arthur.

He embraced her as soon as he was inside, needing to feel her, needing the reassurance that she was all right. "The longest two and a half hours of my life," he rasped into her ear. "If anything had happened to you—"

"The wine is cold," she said. "Why don't you light the candles?"

"This is such a charade," he replied. "I'm too tense to stir up any spirits."

She wrapped her arms around his neck and ran her fingers through his hair. "Concentrate. Wine. Candlelight. Me." Her lips, coaxing, teased his until he could no longer resist kissing her.

Several kisses later, they lit the candles and decanted the wine. They ate by candlelight. They danced to slow mellow music, smooching like teenagers at a prom. Finally, as they danced, she urged him down the hallway to her room.

If Arthur was to be roused, surely the insult of a man's presence in Cynthia's room would rouse him.

They kissed. They caressed greedily. Grant cupped her buttocks in his hands and pulled her hard against his crotch. "I liked you better in that shirt when it was the only thing you had on."

"That could be—"

The rest of her reply was swallowed in a cacophony of noise. The very room seemed to be alive as a rushing wind swept through. It whipped the curtains, ruffled the bedding, rattled the drawer pulls and the pictures on the walls. Bluster howled—a piercing, mournful wail.

Gradually the wind and noise coalesced into a single, central entity. Shocked and disbelieving, Grant released Hayley and turned toward the intruder who took shape before his eyes. Horrified, he could only gasp as

Arthur Ramsey raised a shotgun to his shoulder and pointed it at him.

Hayley had become used to the name-calling Arthur, but this appearance was different. Instead of fatherly wrath, the apparition exuded pure malevolence. The stench of evil filled the room, fetid and sickening.

It seemed to Hayley as though the scene in front of her was playing in slow motion. Paralyzed, fascinated, terrified, she stared at the menacing weapon he held—and she split into two people. She saw the scene from two perspectives and reacted to it as if with two minds. The tyrant was her father; it was Arthur Ramsey, a mean-spirited old ghost who nagged at her. The man in the sights of that hideous weapon was Martin, whom she loved more than life itself; he was Grant, who had made sweet love to her all last night. She was Cynthia Ramsey, protected innocent of another generation; she was Hayley, independent and competent, a modern woman of action.

"No-o-o-o!" she screamed, charging toward the evil. And screamed again as a shot rang out, louder than thunder. She fell, grasping her chest as fire exploded inside her, and darkness descended.

"Hayley. Hayley, please." She heard Grant's voice, felt Grant's hands on her, dragging her. She became aware of Grant's arms around her, holding her to his chest, rocking her.

"W-what?" she asked, blinking as the darkness lifted, and Grant's face came into focus. "Grant?"

But he was paralyzed, his gaze transfixed. Mixed with Bluster's piercing wail was the sound of sobbing, the sound of a heart breaking. Arthur Ramsey knelt before them, holding the lifeless form of his daughter Cynthia. On the floor, another lifeless form, translucent but unmistakably human, lay sprawled. There was blood everywhere. It stained the floor, soaked Cynthia's dress, and the shirt of the lifeless man. Arthur Ramsey's sobs filled the room, reverberating in the wood and plaster.

"Cynthia." The name tore from his throat and with that final anguished cry, Arthur Ramsey crumbled, like a burned-out log collapsing into ash. The inert shades of Cynthia and Martin, too, collapsed. The wind returned, a whirlwind this time, which sucked the ashes into a vortex that swirled up and away. In an instant it was gone, leaving in its wake a tomblike stillness.

Gradually, the miasma of evil dissipated. Grant, who'd been squatting, dropped to the floor and landed squarely on his behind. Hayley sank down next to him. Bluster, delighted to find his favorite humans on the floor, ran over to play.

"Hayley!" Grant said urgently, as if suddenly jolted to an awareness of reality. "God, Hayley." Suddenly he was kissing her deeply, imbuing the kiss with all the pent-up emotion of the past few minutes—the horror, the overwhelming fear, the overpowering relief. When he finally lifted his mouth from hers, he leaped up, pulling her with him. "We're getting out of here."

She had to run to keep up with him. It wouldn't have surprised her if he'd shoved her in the truck and driven back to the hotel, but apparently the pier was far enough away for him. The sight of the moonlit water was soothing, as always. Holding Hayley close, he stared at the lake for a long time.

"I didn't believe you. Is it too late to say I'm sorry?"

"It was never that bad before. If it had been, I'd probably have gone as crazy as you thought I was."

"I never thought you were crazy. I thought you had an overactive imagination." He gave a shout of self-deprecating laughter. "I guess the joke's on me."

"At least we know now. All the questions are answered. Cynthia *is* dead." She sighed. "I used to look at that lake and think about how romantic it was, Cynthia and Martin eloping in a rowboat. And now we know they never made it. Cynthia must have known that her father was watching for Martin, but she had no way to warn him."

"Until she had someone sensitive enough to hear her."

"You're sensitive, too. You heard them. The scream, the shots. You just didn't know what you were hearing. God, Grant, we woke them up, and now they're stuck, reliving that horrible tableau over and over."

"We don't know that we woke them up. Maybe they've been here all this time, but no one heard."

Hayley shivered. "That's a chilling thought."

They were quiet a long time before she asked, "Now what do we do?"

"Let's go in and talk over the possibilities," he said.

Cuddled up in Grant's bed with Bluster curled up at their feet, they embarked on an odd conversation. Fits and spurts of dialogue were interspersed with long passages of thoughtful silence. No matter how they attacked the situation, they always arrived at the same bottom line: Hayley's house was haunted, and the ghosts had to be put to rest. And they always arrived at the same question: How?

"In all the ghost stories I've ever read, the ghosts were restless because there was something left unresolved," Hayley said. "And when that 'something' was resolved, the ghost was laid to rest. But in Arthur's case, the 'something' is that he accidentally killed his daughter. And in Cynthia's case, the 'something' is that she knew what was going to happen and was powerless to stop it. And Martin—well, Martin was killed."

Grant pondered that a moment. "So the 'something' in every case revolves around the fact that Arthur killed Cynthia and Martin," he said. "It follows that the only way to put them to rest would be to change that, and that's impossible."

"I wonder," Hayley mused.

"Facts are unchangeable, Hayley. If it were a matter of Martin and Cynthia being restless because they were killed, then just uncovering the murder would work. But we can't rewrite history and have Arthur *un*kill his daughter."

"Why not?"

He looked at her as though she'd finally gone over the edge. "Because it happened. And once something's happened, it can't *un*happen."

"Unless—"

"I don't know what you're thinking, but if you're about to suggest that we try to change history—"

"Grant, tonight, when Arthur held up that gun and you froze, what did it feel like?"

"What the hell do you think it felt like? You said it yourself. I froze. I was scared witless."

"Did you have any sensation that . . . that it was *you* he was aiming at?"

"It was *me* he was aiming out."

Hayley nestled her cheek more snugly against Grant's chest. "For a few seconds, I felt . . . strange."

"I'm not going to like this, am I?" he asked, when she paused.

"Probably not," she admitted. She sensed he was frowning.

"Well, let's hear it anyway," he said.

"I felt like I was two people at once. I saw Arthur and knew he was Arthur, and yet it also felt . . . well, like I was Cynthia, and he was my father."

"What you're describing borders on possession."

"Borders," she echoed. "Maybe. But I wasn't possessed. I mean, I was still me. I just *related* to Cynthia in some very strange way."

"For the record, Ms. Addison, when you jumped in front of that shotgun I lost ten years off my life."

"What do you think would happen if we could keep Arthur from firing that gun?"

"I still don't get where you're coming from—or heading to."

"If I felt tuned in to Cynthia, then it makes sense that someone else could tune in to Arthur. Someone a little bit like him—enough to relate."

"I hope you're excepting present company."

"Don't be silly. What would you have in common with Arthur? But if we did have someone—say, closer to his age. Someone who knows how to use a shot-gun—"

"You're not thinking about—?"

"Why not? He'd help us. I know he would."

"Oh, sure. We'll just go up to Slim and ask if he'd like to be possessed by Arthur Ramsey."

"We could use a little tact, lead into it gently."

"Either way, it's a harebrained idea. He's not a young man, Hayley. If he saw what we saw tonight, he might drop dead of a heart attack."

"Not if he was prepared. There's nothing frail about Slim, Grant. He's tough as nails."

"Okay. Suppose you got him to agree to try to tune in to Arthur Ramsey. What would you hope to accomplish?"

"When I was tuned in to Cynthia, I did what she did because . . . well, I was protecting Martin. But I was protecting you at the same time. But I had a choice. I mean, if I had been prepared, and I had decided *not* to jump in front of the gun, I think I could have stopped.

And if I could have changed what Cynthia did, maybe Slim could choose not to fire that gun. Especially if I talked him out of it."

There was a second of silence before Grant said, "It would never work, Hayley."

"It might."

"It's too dangerous."

There was another silence. "Why don't we let him decide?"

Grant didn't reply.

"We can tell him," Hayley said. "We can explain everything, down to the last detail, and let him decide whether to try it or not."

"He'll tell us we're both nuts."

"That's what you're really afraid of, isn't it?"

The silence this time was painful and awkward. Finally, Hayley slid her arm tighter around his waist and tilted her head back to kiss his jaw. "I know how you feel, Grant. I didn't want to tell anyone, either. I was . . . embarrassed, afraid they'd think I was crazy. It took a lot of guts for me to tell you, and even when I did, you didn't believe me."

"I'm not proud of that," he said miserably.

"Eventually you listened. And you agreed to *do* something about it. Having a haunted house is— It's like having an embarrassing social disease. You don't want to discuss it, but you can't ignore it. You have to deal with it. I think this could work. And face it, we're fresh out of ideas."

"I wouldn't say that."

"You've got a better idea?"

"Yes," he said, rolling onto his side and stretching his leg over hers. "But it has nothing to do with ghosts."

"I'm going to talk to Slim," Hayley said.

Grant stopped nibbling on her neck long enough to say, "*We're* going to talk to Slim."

"Tomorrow. After work."

"You're going to work tomorrow?"

"I have to. I can't let everything pile up." She expected him to argue but, much to her relief, he didn't.

"That leaves us with tonight."

"Tonight?"

"You're not going back to your house. That leaves us with two options. We can stay here, or we can go back to the hotel."

He was using a lot of body language as he spoke. Hayley sighed as he pulled aside the neck of her shirt and kissed a certain little spot along her shoulder that he'd discovered to be particularly vulnerable to erotic persuasion. "I'll have to go to the house in the morning to dress for work, so staying here would be—" he'd found another little spot "—convenient. I don't really... want to ... leave."

"I'm very glad you said that," he said. "And since we're staying—"

"Hmmm?"

"Let's get naked."

"You have a one-track mind," she murmured as he began working on buttons. "I like it."

Much later, on the verge of sleep, he said, "Hayley?"

Half-asleep, she replied, "Hmm?"

"Before we made love the first time, I said that I wasn't offering you forever."

"Wrapped up in pretty ribbons," she murmured.

"You said you weren't looking for forever, because you'd just moved away from your parents' place."

"Mmm-hmm."

"Hayley?"

"Hmm?"

"I want 'forever.'"

"Forever's a long, long time," she said, snuggling closer.

"No matter what happens at your house. I mean, even if you have to tear it down, and I have to sell the bait shop and go back to a nine-to-five."

"One step at a time," she warned.

"Forever," he repeated. "Say it, Hayley."

"Forever," she gasped, when he'd finally stopped kissing her.

They were very near sleep when she whispered his name.

"Hmm?"

"I want pretty ribbons, too."

11

"HAUNTED, EH? WELL, I guess if any man was cantankerous enough to haunt the hereafter, it would be Arthur Ramsey."

Hayley took heart that Slim didn't seem particularly shocked about the possibility of ghosts as she led into her story. Her eyes met Grant's, and he nodded encouragingly. "Then you do believe that it's possible," she pressed. "You believe that ghosts *could* exist?"

"Well, I've never actually seen one," Slim replied. "But I feel Martha with me, and if she's still around, then maybe—"

Curiosity got the best of Hayley. "You *feel* her?"

"Oh, yes, ma'am," Slim said, nodding absently. "All the time. You see, when she found out she was . . . that there wasn't much time left, she told me, 'Now, Slim, don't close me up in a box somewhere. I want you to have me cremated. And one day when you're out in that boat of yours, all by yourself, I want you to sprinkle me on the water. That way I can keep an eye on you when you're out there fishing, and you'll know I'm around when you hear the water slapping against the boat.' And then she laughed, and she said, 'When you clean your fish and throw your fish heads back in the water, you'll know I'm keeping count.'"

He fell into a reflective silence for several seconds. Then he nodded again. "Yes, ma'am. I feel her. She's there, as sure as the water's there and the fish are swimming in it and the sun's ashining on it."

Hayley had to choke back a lump in her throat. "That's sweet."

"Well, the ghost we're talking about is not so sweet," Grant warned.

"Old Arthur was ornery when he was alive," Slim said. "I don't expect dying would improve his disposition."

Hayley looked at Grant again. He squeezed her hand. "Go ahead."

She'd told Slim only that Arthur Ramsey had harassed her. Now she told him the rest of the story, just as she had related it to Grant. She showed him the poem, pointed out the hearts, and told him about Cynthia's visit, then concluded with, "That's when Grant and I decided to try to find out what really happened on the night Cynthia and Martin eloped."

Grant took up the story, related their plan to rouse Arthur, and described the chain of events after Arthur appeared.

"That's some story," Slim said, and for a moment, no one spoke. Finally, he shifted restlessly. "Well, there's got to be a reason you've told me all this. Let's have it."

Hayley explained the way she'd been able to feel Cynthia's emotions, and put forth her theory that if they could stop Arthur from killing Cynthia and Martin, then the ghosts could be put to rest. "We—myself, mostly—Grant's not thrilled with the whole idea—

thought that if you could tune in to Arthur, then I might be able to stop him from firing the gun."

"You don't have to do it," Grant added. "If you have any reservations—"

"And we don't know that it would work if you do," Hayley admitted.

"We'll never know if we don't try," Slim said.

"You'll do it?" Hayley hadn't realized how afraid she'd been that he'd refuse.

They mapped out a plan.

"I still don't like the gun," Grant said, as they drove from Slim's house to the bait shop in Hayley's car. "If Arthur had had a real gun last night, you'd be history. I've never seen so much blood."

"I wondered why Agnes O'Keefe carpeted that room. I'd be willing to bet that if we pulled back the carpet, we'd find bloodstains in the wood. Can you imagine what it must have been like for Arthur to live in that house knowing Cynthia's blood was there?"

"We all know he went totally bonkers," Grant said. "Which is exactly what the idea of bringing a real gun into that room is."

Hayley looked at Slim and frowned. "Would you please reassure him again, Slim?"

"Unloaded it myself," Slim said. "You watched me. We double-checked. Hell, we triple-checked. I don't even have any shells with me."

Grant's answer was a lockjawed scowl.

"It'll be easier for us to stop him if we have something tangible to grab," Hayley said. "I don't know what would happen if I touched the ghost weapon.

When I threw the swan at Arthur, it went straight through him." She shivered. "Let's get it right the first time. I don't want to have to try more than once."

"We aren't going to try more than once," Grant stated grimly. "It's tonight or never."

At the house, Hayley showed Slim to her bedroom, and left him sitting on the edge of the bed, the shotgun on one side of him, a pile of magazines on the other. Pausing in the doorway, she raised her hand, showing him crossed fingers for luck. He responded with a grin and a thumbs-up sign.

Grant had already turned on the stereo by the time she returned to the living room. He tried to smile, but didn't quite succeed as he held out his arms. "Care to dance?"

They moved stiffly at first. "This was difficult enough last night, before I knew what was coming."

"Just try to forget everything but us," she said. "It's the emotion that stirs him up. You're so tense."

"Maybe if you were a little closer—"

"Maybe if you kissed my neck a little—"

"You smell good. And you taste—I think I'm feeling a little emotional."

"I noticed."

"There are some natural phenomena that can't be squelched, even by a ghost."

"If Arthur Ramsey squelches *this* natural phenomenon, he'll have me to answer to." She patted the phenomenon in question. "It's private property."

"Hayley, kiss me."

The seriousness of his tone stopped her in midstep. She looked questioningly into his eyes.

"I need you close to me right now," he said, tightening his arms around her. His rough kiss expressed all the raw need and apprehension boiling inside him.

In response to his need, she soothed him with gentle strokes of her fingertips, over his face, his ears, his scalp. She sprinkled kisses on his cheeks and eyelids.

"I'm quivering inside, and you're calm as Mount Rushmore," he said, burying his face between her breasts.

"Trust me, I'm quivering."

"After tonight, I don't want you quivering over anything but me."

He kissed her again, and when he finally drew away, she whispered, "I think it's time we adjourned to the bedroom."

Arms across each other's back, they walked down the hall, each hoping they would never do so with such dread again.

They didn't acknowledge Slim's presence, nor did he acknowledge theirs as he carried the shotgun to the designated spot in the center of the room.

"This isn't easy with an audience," Hayley said, as Grant kissed her neck.

"I'm having problems concentrating, too," Grant admitted. "But I'll tell you one thing, Hayley Addison—if we get rid of your ghosts and there's still breath in our bodies, we're going to do what Cynthia Ramsey and Martin Bertram tried to do almost fifty years ago."

She looked at him in wide-eyed surprise. "Elope? Grant, I couldn't do that to my family. There's no need to. They're going to love you."

"The question is, do you love me? Don't look at me like that. You've never said it."

"Of course, I love you," she said.

"Then I don't care how we do it, as long as we do it soon. I want you to be part of my life. And I want it official."

Hayley felt like sighing, laughing, shouting his name, hugging him and kissing him, all at the same time. Her heart sang with her love for him. Her body ached to join with his.

Grant felt what she was feeling in the way her body pressed against his. He saw it in her eyes, and heard it in her ragged breathing.

And Arthur Ramsey honed in on that emotion like radar on a vibration. His arrival was accompanied by all the tumult and confusion of the night before.

Hayley watched, detached and yet a part of it. She saw Arthur Ramsey holding the gun, raising it, sighting, but he was also Slim. The man next to her was Grant, but he was also Martin Bertram. She was Hayley, but she was also Cynthia. And she was fighting for her life, and for the life of the man she loved.

"No!" she cried, lunging forward. Grant was beside her, moving in unison with her. They both reached for the barrel of the shotgun, but it was Grant, with his superior strength, who managed to shove it upward just in time.

A shot discharged harmlessly toward the ceiling. Arthur—Slim—glowered at them, a murderous gleam in his crazed eyes. He and Grant struggled as Arthur tried to lower the barrel. With youth on his side, Grant managed to keep it high.

"Arthur, stop!" Hayley argued desperately. "Cynthia loves this man. You don't want to kill the man she loves. You don't want to hurt Cynthia."

"Cynthia!"

The cry came with such force that it rattled the windows. "Don't make her choose between you," Hayley pleaded. "She loves you both. If you accept the man she loves, then you won't lose her."

"Cynthia!" Tears glistened on Arthur's cheeks. He was no longer fighting.

"Let go of the gun," Hayley urged. "It'll only cause you sorrow."

With a wrenching sob, Arthur released the gun. Grant heaved a sigh of relief as he took the weapon and lowered it.

"Cynthia," Arthur sobbed again.

Hayley hugged him. "You never have to give her up now."

"Cynthia," he repeated, still sobbing, and Hayley felt Grant's hand grasp hers and pull her away.

The next thing she knew, she was wrapped in his arms, being gently rocked back and forth. Slim had stepped back, too, and Arthur's ghost was translucent.

"Look," Hayley whispered, awed by the scene being enacted by the ghostly trio. Cynthia was embracing

Arthur, just as Hayley had. Martin was holding her hand, just as Grant had taken Hayley's. And Arthur had his hand on Martin's shoulder in a gesture of acceptance.

Their shapes faded slowly, with none of the violence that had characterized their arrival. The last remaining image was that of the teardrops on Arthur's cheeks; those drops lingered in the air, sparkling like diamonds in sunlight, and then disappeared in a single twinkle of light.

Instead of the stench of evil, the scent of gardenias wafted in the air, delicate and benign.

The atmosphere in the room felt as though it had been cleansed. The silence that descended was full and rich and filled with peace. For a long moment no one moved or spoke.

"I'll . . . be . . . damned!" Slim said finally.

"It worked," Grant said. Then, picking Hayley up and swinging her in circles, he said it again, joyously. "It worked!"

"It worked," Hayley echoed, catching his jubilation, laughing and crying at the same time. "Arthur's gone."

She was dizzy when Grant put her down, but after regaining her equilibrium, she went over to Slim and gave him a hug. "We couldn't have done it without you."

"Wouldn't have missed it for the world," Slim replied. "A man gets my age, there aren't many surprises or new experiences. Wait'll I tell Martha."

"There's a bottle of wine left over from last night. What do you gentlemen say to a drink?"

With a chorus of, "Hear, hear!" and, "Prosit!" they meandered down the hall. Bluster trotted along behind, bouncing with excitement.

They were giddy with relief, and laughed and clinked their glasses together dramatically like characters in a glitzy forties movie. Grant made the first toast. "To an *un*haunted house, and the woman who lives there!"

Hayley offered the next salute. "To Cynthia and Martin—may they find in death what life denied them!"

"To Arthur Ramsey—may he rest in peace!" Slim said.

Relief, wine and the late hour mellowed them. On the second round of toasts, Grant put his arm across Hayley's shoulders possessively and said, "To love."

Tears welled in his eyes as he looked down into Hayley's face and they clinked glasses. When they extended their arms to touch their glasses to Slim's, Grant said, "I don't know if you heard in the bedroom, Slim. Hayley and I are getting married."

"Then this one's to a rosy future," Slim proposed.

"You don't seem very surprised," Grant commented.

"Humph!" Slim retorted. "I knew it the first day I met you two."

"But we were barely speaking that day," Hayley said.

Slim chortled. "What has talking got to do with it? Never seen two young people trying so hard not to notice each other."

Suddenly Bluster went into a frenzy of barking, baying and whining. At the back door he jumped and scratched at the doorjamb.

Panicked, Hayley looked from Grant to Slim. "The only time he acts like that . . . You don't think—?"

They dashed to the door, opened it and followed Bluster out into the Florida room. From the direction of the lake came the sound of laughter. Through the screen walls of the porch they watched in stunned silence as Martin Bertram helped Cynthia Ramsey into a rowboat. She gained her footing and, still holding her hands, Martin leaned forward to kiss her gently before stepping into the boat with her.

"Wait!"

At the cry, Cynthia and Martin turned their heads toward the source. Arthur Ramsey stepped out of the shadows in the yard and stalked toward the boat.

Hayley held her breath, and felt Grant's fingers tighten tensely where they rested on her shoulder. Slim, too, was still and tense. The three people on the patio scarcely breathed as they waited for what would happen next.

Arthur extended his right hand to Martin. Martin took it, and they engaged in a hearty handshake. Then Arthur turned his attention to Cynthia and held out his hands. She reached up and placed hers in them, and tilted her cheek for a kiss as Arthur bent forward. They shared a quick, impulsive hug before she turned back to Martin.

When she and Martin were seated, facing each other, Martin picked up the oars, pushed off from the pier, and began rowing. As the boat and its passengers moved soundlessly over the water, the moonlight spilling over them created a romantic tableau. Just before they floated out of sight, Cynthia and Martin waved to Arthur Ramsey, who waved back with broad sweeps of his arm. "Godspeed!"

The word echoed across the empty lake. The boat had vanished, and so had Arthur Ramsey.

With her shoulders resting against Grant's broad chest, Hayley said, "They're gone for good this time."

Slim nodded absently. "Arthur's made his peace."

"After all this time," Grant added, and then mused, "What do you suppose he did with the bodies?"

"I've been giving that a little thought myself," Slim said. "Of course, with the lake outside, a body would present no problem. Just weight it down, and the fish and turtles would take care of the rest."

Hayley shivered. "Not a pretty thought. No, I don't think he would have done that to Cynthia."

"I didn't say he threw Cynthia in the lake," Slim said, staring out at the lawn. "I always thought it was peculiar that an ornery old man like Arthur Ramsey would baby a bunch of gardenia bushes the way he did."

"You mean?"

Slim shrugged. "Where better for his daughter than surrounded by the flowers she loved?"

Hayley twisted her head to look at Grant. "Should we check?"

"What good would it do anyone?"

"There could be authorities we should notify."

"To what end?"

"For the record, I agree with Grant," Slim said. "What good would it do to move her if she's there? Her father tended her grave for nigh on to forty years—what more loving tribute could she have had?"

Hayley turned to slip her arms around Grant's waist and rest her cheek on his chest. "I guess we'll never know for sure."

Slim shifted restlessly. "Well, kids, it's late for this old warrior. It's been a big night, but I'd kinda like to get home."

"I'll get my keys," Hayley offered.

"No," Slim said. "Grant, if you'll loan me your little putt-putt, I think I'd like to go home on the water tonight."

"Are you sure?" Grant asked. "It doesn't have much of a light, although I can loan you a lantern."

"The moon's full," Slim replied. "Besides, I'd know my way home on this lake with my eyes closed. To tell you the truth, I'd like to have a little chat with Martha on the way."

Cradling Bluster in her arms, Hayley watched from the porch while Grant accompanied Slim to the pier and helped him push off. When he returned, he greeted Hayley with a brief kiss, then stretched his arm across her shoulders.

"It's really over," she said, as they watched the small motorboat disappear around the bend.

"For Arthur," Grant agreed. "For us, it's really just beginning."

Hayley sighed. "I'd like to think that it's just begin-ning for Cynthia and Martin, too. Finally."

"Who can say?" He gave her shoulders a gentle squeeze. "Right now, I want to focus on us."

She twisted slightly to look him in the eye. "Let's go inside."

"Your place or mine?"

Her gaze was unflinching as she told him, "I want to make love with you in my bed, in my house."

He was more than happy to oblige. And they dis-covered that the sensual magic was as strong in her bedroom as it had been in the back of the bait shop and at the hotel.

As they lay together under the covers in the after-glow of their lovemaking, Grant said, "No signs of Ar-thur."

"It's not Arthur's house anymore," Hayley replied. "Now it's ours."

"Ours and you-know-who's," Grant reminded, as Bluster plopped onto the foot of the bed and searched for a cozy spot to settle.

"*He's* ours, too," she said. "We've always had joint custody."

"I suppose so," Grant agreed, snuggling deeper into the pillow.

"Were you surprised when Slim said what he said about us?" Hayley asked.

"What? That he knew about us the first time he saw us together?"

"Mmm-hmm."

"No."

She rolled over so that they were face-to-face on the pillow. "You weren't?"

"No."

"Why?"

"Because as soon as he said it, I realized that I had known it, too."

"Even then?"

"Why do you think I was trying so hard not to be nice to you? I knew I had one foot in the air and the other on a banana peel, where you were concerned." Grinning, he added, "You were trying just as hard not to notice me. Admit it—didn't you know something special was about to happen?"

Hayley thought back to the first time she'd seen him—the way she'd admired, from afar, the way he moved and the way he filled out his jeans. She rolled so that he couldn't see her face. "No," she said, smiling smugly. "I didn't have an inkling."

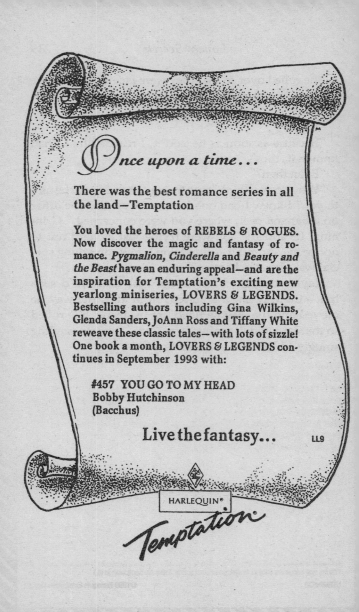